DEAD REAL

A totally addictive crime thriller with a huge twist

HELEN H. DURRANT

DI Calladine & DS Bayliss Book 12

JOFFE
BOOKS

Joffe Books, London
www.joffebooks.com

First published in Great Britain in 2022

ISBN: 978-1-80405-402-4

To Shelley, with lots of love on the occasion of her fiftieth birthday.

PROLOGUE

A screech of brakes, the van skidded to a halt and Noah Crosby jumped out. A quick wave to his mate, then he made for the Pheasant pub a couple of hundred metres away. He was only sixteen but the new landlord, 'Mad Mick', wasn't fussy. In it for the money and sod the law. A lot like himself.

He and his mate had done over the late-night shop on the Oldston Road. It'd been profitable too. He had a pocket full of cash and plenty of cigarettes stashed away that he'd sell later.

"Hey, laddie — a word."

The voice came from the shadow of the tower block. For a brief moment, Noah thought he recognised it, but it couldn't be, not in this hell hole in the middle of the night. "What you after? Got a load of ciggies for sale but that's it," he called back. "I'm all out of dope."

"Who're you working for, that rogue Spooner? Sends you out to do the dirty work, does he, then takes all the cream. Talented lad like you, I'm surprised."

Noah walked over to the figure. He couldn't make him out properly. The man was dressed in dark clothing and had a cap pulled down low over his face making him difficult to recognise. "Why're you so interested?"

"That's my business. Tell me where to find him."

Noah punched his arm. "Tell you anything and I'm dead."

"Bright lad like you, I'm surprised you work for that thug."

People didn't criticise Ricky Spooner — or Spook to give him his street name — and get away with it. He had eyes and ears everywhere and some powerful backup. The world thought him legit, but Noah reckoned he knew better. "Me and Spook are done," he sneered. "But I'd be careful. Spook gets wind that you're dissing his good name and you won't live out the day. Who are you anyway?"

Noah looked intently at what he could see of the man's face. He didn't know him so he had to be new.

The man laughed. "If you don't work for Spooner, it's got to be the other one, Barton."

"Not a chance. If I were you I'd get lost while you still can. I don't know what your game is but neither Spook or Barton like strange faces sticking their noses in."

Warning delivered, Noah swaggered off towards the Pheasant with a grin on his face. Spook owed him one.

The man came up behind him. "Sorry, kid. I've waited long enough, now someone's going to pay."

Noah had no idea what he meant, but he had better things to do than listen to half arsed threats from some no mark. "Get lost while you've still got the use of your legs."

Amused at the man's nerve, Noah continued towards the pub. A second later he felt a searing pain in his back. He sank to his knees. The knife hadn't gone in deep but the wound was bad enough to have him gasping for breath. Noah felt the man grab his hair and pull his head back.

"Leave me," he rasped.

"Sorry, lad, no can do." For a long moment the man stared deep into his eyes. "You have no idea, do you? D'you even know who I am?"

All the lad could do was blink, puzzled. He wanted to say something, beg for his life, but he was incapable of uttering a word. Seconds later, he was spitting, choking on his own blood.

The man drew the blade slow and deep across Noah Crosby's throat.

CHAPTER ONE

Three weeks later

Tuesday

Over the years the alleyway that ran between two of the tower blocks had become a dumping ground for rubbish. It was littered with old mattresses, fridges, anything the tenants didn't want and couldn't afford to have disposed of properly.

Lisa Woodley, single mum of two and new to the area, lived in a ground floor flat in Heron House, one of the pair of towers. A week ago she'd complained about the smell. The council promised to send a team round to shift everything within a couple of days. All very well but the days were passing by, the weather was warm and the smell got no better.

The Hobfield estate was not an easy place to live in. After dark the kids were noisy. They let off fireworks late into the night and screamed obscenities at everyone who walked past. They kept the children awake and made Lisa flinch. The smell was the final straw. She'd had enough.

Lisa planned to visit the council offices in Leesdon that afternoon, give them a piece of her mind. She was all fired up and ready to take them on when 'Bobbin', her cat, came home with a human foot in his mouth. The animal dropped it on the kitchen floor, looked up at Lisa and went to his basket where he began to lick his paws.

* * *

"Looks okay, doesn't he?" said DC Simon Rockliffe, known affectionately as 'Rocco' to his colleagues. "Two months off has done him good."

DS Ruth Bayliss nodded. "He's lost weight, goes to the gym these days too. Who'd have thought it, our slobby leader actually took his doctor's advice. Mind you, I think it has more to do with Kitty than anyone else. She's the one who's taken him in hand."

"They're definitely an item then?" Rocco said.

"Looks very much like it. These last couple of months Kitty Lake has featured in his life big style. She was even his plus one at my wedding. Caused a flurry of gossip that did. A lot of women had their claws out, particularly Monika — remember her, Tom's old flame? She didn't stop staring daggers at the pair all night."

Rocco grinned. Calladine's love-life was always guaranteed to add a little light relief to the working day. "Is he back full time then?"

"So he reckons. Greco said he could ease his way in but you know Tom, he actually misses the place — and us too of course." Ruth grinned back.

Rocco looked towards the glass panels that walled off DI Tom Calladine's office. He was sitting, head down at his desk, eyes glued to paperwork. Two months ago he'd collapsed in front of them, right here in the main office. It'd given them all a hellava scare. The way he looked that day, the grey pallor of his face, spoke of a heart attack, and Rocco had doubted the boss would be back. But it had been a false alarm. A *change your ways or else* warning, and Calladine had heeded it.

"He doesn't want treating with kid gloves either. He made that plain enough at the weekend when I saw him," Ruth said.

"But we can't pretend it didn't happen," Rocco dropped his voice. "Has he mentioned retirement?" he mouthed to Ruth.

"No, and don't you dare," she snapped back. "He's only fifty-two and intends to carry on for a few years yet."

"If it was me I'd be out and doing something else. Don't misunderstand me, I love the job and want promotion, but there comes a time when enough is enough. And come on, Ruth, Leesdon's not an easy watch, is it? The Hobfield sees to that."

Ruth was about to add her own slant to the argument when the office phone rang. Rocco grabbed it. It was the duty sergeant from downstairs.

"Problem, Rocco," he began. "And a nasty one. A human foot found on the Hobfield. You know what that means."

Indeed he did. Some poor soul had fallen foul of whichever villain was currently running the estate and had been made an example of. Proof, if they needed it, of what he'd just said to Ruth. This town was no picnic to police. Calladine should have run while he had the chance.

CHAPTER TWO

DI Tom Calladine had missed any number of things during his absence but he hadn't missed the Hobfield. He stood, grim faced, looking up at the tower blocks looming above him, reflecting on the mayhem they'd brought his way over the years.

Doctor Natasha Barrington, lead pathologist from the Duggan Centre, was in attendance. She went over to join him. "Good to see you back, Tom. Shame about the circumstances though. I had planned a more civilised catch-up over a drink."

Calladine smiled. "Perhaps when this is sorted. What have you got?"

"Julian's CSI team found the body of a young male only minutes after starting a search of the alley over there."

'Julian' was Professor Julian Batho, head of forensic science at the Duggan. "Any idea how long he's been there?" Calladine asked.

"Difficult to say, with the warm weather decomposition is advanced. The maggots are having a field day and the wildlife's been at him. Fingers nibbled, the detached foot we know about and chunks are missing from his arms and legs too. Rats, I reckon."

Calladine's stomach churned. This place got no better.

She handed him three evidence bags: one contained a gym membership card, another a flashy-looking gold watch and the last a mobile phone. "We have a lead on who he is too. The card was in a plastic wallet in his hoodie pocket which protected it. As you can see, his name is Noah. There's no surname on the card, so not much help there. We'll get forensics and communications onto the phone. It could prove informative."

Calladine nodded. "I know that gym. When we've finished here I'll pay them a visit. I'm sure they'll be able to tell me who he is, er, was." Once he had a full name he'd get DC Alice Bolshaw to do a background check back at the station.

Natasha held up the bag containing the gold watch. "This was on his wrist. Looks the business and an unusual design, plus the mobile is top of the range, so I presume the motive wasn't robbery."

Calladine took a photo of the card and the watch with his phone, donned a set of paper overalls, gloves and a mask and followed Natasha into the alley, with Ruth trailing in their wake.

"It's not pretty, Tom. The body was wrapped in an old sheet, pushed under a discarded table and bags of rubbish piled up around it. Given the state of the alleyway, if he'd been killed in the winter months he could have lain there for ages. He has a deep wound to his throat. I'll know more when I get him back to the morgue."

"Murder then?"

"Looks like it."

Calladine picked his way carefully through the rubbish over to the body. Noah Crosby lay on his back. Half his face had been eaten away by maggots. His eyes were missing and most of his mouth, leaving his teeth exposed in a parody of a hideous grin.

"The sheet has holes in it and his clothing is in shreds," Natasha said. "I'll do all the checks but I reckon it's due to determined wildlife trying to get at the flesh."

"Rubbish tip or not, I'm surprised he wasn't found before now."

Ruth said from behind him, "Look at it, Tom. No one walks up here. It's blocked solid with all the stuff folk can't be bothered to take to the dump — bin bags, old white goods. The ground is littered with broken glass and pitch black at night, besides it only leads to the rough ground at the back."

"She's right, Tom," Natasha said. "If it hadn't been for the woman on the ground floor of Heron House complaining about the smell, and then today her cat . . . well, you know the rest."

Fair enough. No one looked too closely at anything on the Hobfield, afraid of what they'd find. "What's happening on the estate these days, place still run by hooligans dealing dope?"

"We suspect there's currently a battle going on between two different gangs," Ruth said. "One run by a Ricky Spooner, aka Spook, a young man new to villainy, and the other a local lad, Luke Barton. Both are in their early twenties and each of them is trying to run this estate. Barton we know about, he has history, but Spooner is more of a question mark. The reality is there's not enough intel on either of them. So far we haven't found anything concrete to charge them with. We're pretty sure that anyone we've caught with drugs or knives recently will be working for one or the other but they're always tight-lipped, even going so far as to take the rap for whichever one they're working for. Both Spook and Barton play things close and don't suffer loose talk is what we're told. The punishment for squealing is harsh." She nodded at the body.

"You're thinking this is a case in point?" Calladine said.

"Could be. On the plus side all's been quiet this last fortnight," Ruth said. "No one's got beaten up, shot or ended up in hospital due to injecting something cut with rubbish. From which I can only presume that both gangs have their enterprises running like clockwork."

"You reckon this poor bugger crossed one of them? Do we know which gang he worked for?" Calladine said.

"No, but knowing his full name will help."

Calladine left the alleyway and went to find Rocco. "I want you to ask around, speak to people and find out what's happening around here. That lad upset someone. He was possibly running drugs for one of the two thugs Ruth mentioned. If that's the case, I want a name."

Ruth followed Calladine out. She nudged him. "No one's going to talk to him, particularly not the kids. But at a pinch they might talk to me."

Calladine grinned. He couldn't help it. "You say this lot are so tight-lipped, so what special power have you got?"

She nodded at a single storey building next to the tower blocks. "I've been helping Jake run the youth club at the community centre over there. The kids are age twelve to eighteen, boys and girls. They're a rough bunch and as far as we know not involved in the dealing, though even I can't be sure. But slowly they're beginning to trust us. I steer the conversation the right way and I might learn something."

"Do they know you're a copper?" Calladine asked.

"I don't broadcast it but I suspect they do. I just go along occasionally to help out. But they do like Jake and seem to trust him. He acquired some new IT equipment for the centre, he got a grant and had the place kitted out. That's made him 'Mr Popular', the kids reckon he's okay."

"Can I come along?" Calladine asked.

"You can come tonight if you're free. But you keep it simple, we're all on first name terms, keep the chat light and don't ask too many questions, leave that to me or Jake. If the kids get the idea you're fishing, you'll get nowt."

Calladine nodded. "Change of plan, Rocco. Ruth and I will go and check out the gym, see what they can tell us about our victim. You get back to the station and bring the team up to speed. I want whatever information we've got on both Spooner and Barton."

* * *

The gym Noah had attended was on the High Street behind the supermarket. "This is where I come," Calladine told Ruth. "Twice a week, Monday and Thursday. Miss a session and Kitty makes my life a misery." He patted his stomach. "It's worth it though. The exercise, the diet, it's not taken long to get me back in shape."

"Make sure you don't slip back into your old ways," she warned. "I don't want a repeat performance of what happened that day."

"Me neither, don't you worry." Calladine knew his collapse had terrified his team, and particularly Ruth. They were close friends as well as colleagues.

At the main desk he showed the gym receptionist his badge and gave her a big smile. "Sorry, Jodie, this is police business. We're interested in a young man called Noah who comes here. We don't know his surname. Can you help us?"

"We only have one Noah, Mr Calladine, but I haven't seen him in a while." She checked the computer. "The last time he was here was four weeks ago."

That fitted the timescale. "Could you give us his full name and address, possibly a photo we could have?"

She tapped away on her keyboard. "This is him, Noah Crosby. I'll print out his details for you."

Calladine took a look at the image on the membership record. It was difficult to tell given the state of the body, but the hair looked the same. "No other members called Noah?"

"No, he's it. What's happened to him?"

"I can't say, not until we've spoken to his family."

Jodie looked concerned. "It's bad then, shame. When he did come here he kept himself to himself. On the rare occasions we spoke he mentioned his mother, said they both live on that rough estate, the one at the other end of town."

That didn't surprise Calladine. The Hobfield, exactly where they'd just come from.

CHAPTER THREE

Jodie was right, Noah had lived with his mother, Anna Crosby. Their home was the middle house in a row of ten on the edge of the estate.

"On a lovely day like today and with those trees in blossom, this part of the Hobfield doesn't look that bad," Ruth said.

"A few trees and the odd sunny afternoon won't change this place." Calladine's reply was jaundiced. He'd been dealing with trouble on this estate far too long to be swayed by appearances. He knocked on the front door of the Crosby house and immediately a neighbour's dog began to bark.

A woman called to them from inside. "You the electrician? Only you were supposed to ring first."

"We're the police," Calladine called back. "We need a word."

The pair heard a number of bolts being drawn, a key in a latch, then finally a small blonde woman peered nervously around the door. "Sorry about all the security but you can't be too careful around here."

Calladine showed her his badge. "We're here about Noah."

Her face fell. She stood to one side and ushered them in, locking the door, bolts and all, behind her. "He's not got himself into more bother, has he? That boy gives me nothing but worry these days. I did think he'd settle when he got that job. So much for that."

"When did you last see him?" Ruth asked.

"A while back. He comes and goes does our Noah. He'll be staying with one of his mates. He'll come home when he's fed up."

"How long is a while, Mrs Crosby?" Ruth asked.

She shrugged but gave it some thought. "Perhaps a month."

Calladine checked the details from the gym. "He's only sixteen, weren't you concerned about him?" he asked gently. To his mind this amount of freedom was excessive for one so young.

"Noah doesn't appreciate me fussing. Living round here and having no dad, he's had to grow up fast."

Noah's mum led them into the small sitting room. Calladine held out his mobile and showed her the image of the watch. "D'you recognise this?"

"It belongs to Noah, he bought it a while ago." She looked at them, her eyes suddenly full of questions she didn't want to ask. "He always wore it on his wrist. Didn't feel dressed without it. I don't understand, how come you've got a photo of it?"

He showed her the image of the gym record. "And this?"

"Yes, that's him." She looked from one to the other of them, growing worry evident on her face. "What's happened? It must be something bad to bring you lot to my door."

"I'm afraid we've found a body on the estate and we believe it to be Noah. His gym membership card was found in his pocket and the watch was on his wrist."

Noah's mother sat down hard in an armchair, shaking her head. "No, you're wrong. It won't be Noah, he's far too careful. I warned him, he knows what it's like round here and who to avoid. He doesn't like trouble."

"Warned him about who, Mrs Crosby?" Ruth asked.

Noah's mother tried to shrug this off. "You know what this estate is like. There are plenty of ruffians who try to take advantage. My Noah has a mouth on him, gives as good as he gets, and that doesn't always go down well."

"He wasn't being bothered by anyone in particular then?" Ruth asked.

Noah's mother shook her head. "No, of course not. That's not what I meant."

"D'you have any idea who might have harmed him?" Ruth asked.

Noah's mum shook her head vigorously. "No. If I did, I'd tell you."

"You said Noah had a job," Ruth said. "Where exactly?"

"It was nothing special, a few hours a week at Goddard's — you know, the garden centre in Hopecross."

Ruth made a note. They'd have to visit, find out when they'd last seen him.

"Okay, his identity will be confirmed with a DNA test but you should prepare yourself. The victim is more than likely your son," Calladine told her.

"Why can't I just visit the morgue to identify him? I have to see him for myself, make sure whoever you've found is my Noah."

There was no way he could let her go through that. "I don't think that's a good idea. But I'll discuss it with my colleagues at the morgue and let you know."

Her fearful eyes searched Calladine's face for what he wasn't telling her. "What're you keeping from me? You're keeping something."

He coughed. "Noah had been left wrapped in the open for some time. What with the warm weather . . ."

She nodded and then burst into tears. "Bodies don't keep in this weather. That's what you mean, isn't it? I'm not stupid. He was killed and dumped somewhere, poor sod."

Calladine left her, weeping, with Ruth and went out into the hallway. He was going to take a quick look at the lad's room. Noah might not have lived at home but Calladine was after anything that would help them understand why he had been killed.

He went up the stairs and into a small bedroom. There was nothing obvious to see. Everything was neat and tidy but a more thorough search might throw up something. Calladine pulled open a cupboard drawer — nothing but socks, and the others were empty. The woman was telling the truth, her son didn't live here.

Calladine returned to the sitting room. "Can you recall when he last slept here?"

"Not for a while," his mother replied. "But he knows the room's ready, should he want it."

"Can I ask you to leave his room as it is? We'll have to carry out a thorough search," Calladine said.

"You've had one huge shock. Is there anyone who can come and sit with you?" Ruth asked. "What about Noah's dad?"

"He's long gone, love. Anyway, I don't need anyone," she insisted. "This is a mistake, I know it. If Noah was dead I'd feel it. He's not perfect, he knows some dodgy people, but he wouldn't be stupid enough to get himself killed."

"Has Noah ever been in trouble with the police?" Ruth asked.

"Not really. The odd telling off but no more than most lads on this estate."

"D'you know who his friends are, who he would stay with when he's not at home?" Ruth asked.

"He and Dean Seddon were close once. He might know something." She looked up at the detectives. "He isn't a bad lad, but he didn't choose his friends wisely. Dean's okay but some of the others are nothing but fledgling gangsters and they lead my Noah astray."

"Do they have names?" Calladine asked.

She shook her head. "Just lads, and anyway, I prefer to keep out of Noah's business. He knows not to overstep the mark, I've warned him often enough."

Given the lad's age, Calladine doubted that. "We'll be in touch," he said, and stood up.

"You look very pale," Ruth said. "I think you should have someone with you."

"Glynis from next door. Fetch her."

* * *

"He must have been sleeping elsewhere," Calladine said on their way to the car. "What we need to know now is where. This Dean Seddon. D'you know the name?"

"He comes to the centre sometimes but he's hard to like. He might have been pally with Noah at one time but lately I haven't seen him with anyone I know. Dean is fast turning into a young thug who spends too much time with Ricky Spooner. The Spooner family have that car showroom off the bypass. They employ any number of youngsters to valet the cars, it's possible Dean's just another one."

Calladine shook his head. "I've only been gone two months, how come the swift turnover of villains?"

"A lot of the old ones are no longer with us. They're either languishing in a prison cell or dead. The younger element spotted a gap and filled it."

Calladine sighed. Wasn't it always the way?

"Because of alleged drug dealing, Barton has been on uniform's radar for a while, Tom, but with no proof that he's involved, CID had no reason to look into his activities."

"Well, perhaps it's about time we did, but let's find this Dean Seddon first and see what he can tell us."

Back in the car, Calladine rang Alice Bolshaw at the station and asked her to look up Seddon's address and any background they had. She was back to them within minutes.

"He lives at flat ten on floor three of Heron House with his mother and older brother. The brother, Killian, was up on a charge of dealing last summer but he got off, insufficient evidence. According to the report the officer who stopped him for speeding saw a suspicious looking package on the passenger seat of the car. Knowing the Seddon brothers' reputation he wanted to question him further, assuming it to be drugs."

16

"Why didn't the officer look?" Calladine asked.

"It's not that simple, sir. Killian got out of the car and both he and the officer were set upon by two men and clobbered on the head. When they came round, the package was gone. The officer spent several days in hospital with concussion and couldn't recall much. When he was finally able to relate what happened, he was so unsure of events that Killian's solicitor considered his statement unsafe. His lawyer was concerned that a colleague keen to make an arrest had suggested to the officer that there were drugs in the car."

"Were the assailants caught?"

"No, sir, and no one saw anything either."

CHAPTER FOUR

"What's he like, this Seddon?" Calladine asked from the passenger seat.

"He's okay, very different from Dean. He's eighteen but he still comes to the community centre. He helps the younger ones set up their own blogs and websites, and he's doing well given his past."

"Alice said he's got history."

"Since the attack on his brother he's not been the same. He's less aggressive and I doubt he's into dealing dope anymore," Ruth said.

Calladine pulled a face. "I'm getting too old for all this. Things change so quick around here these days, I can't keep up with the new names and faces."

"You've been off sick and missed a lot. Give yourself chance," Ruth came back. "You don't recognise a few names, so what? They're the new boys on the estate. I only know some of them because of the centre."

"Kitty keeps telling me that if I get too bogged down there's always retirement."

"Over the years you've put your heart and soul into keeping this town trouble free, so don't start with the feeling sorry for yourself drivel. And what's Kitty doing filling you head full of ideas like that? You love your job. The station and the team wouldn't be the same without you."

"Kitty's not the only one, Zoe thinks I should seriously consider it too."

"Zoe is lining you up for child care, that's all. She's got baby Maisie now, and with a business to run she needs all the help she can get. A solicitor's lot is not an easy one."

Calladine knew Ruth was right. His daughter, Zoe, and her partner, Jo, were finding combining work with parenthood hard. "Right then, let's go and see what the Seddons have to say for themselves."

Ruth pulled out onto the main road. "What's Kitty up to these days? I presume the world of private investigating is keeping her busy?"

"She's embroiled in something new but doesn't say much and I don't pry. Got enough of my own to think about."

"Doesn't she ask for your help?" Ruth said.

"She asks for my opinion sometimes, that's about all. Whether she takes much notice is another matter." He shrugged. "We don't live in each other's pockets, you know. Officially her address is the flat above her office, not my cottage."

"But she stays with you most of the time."

"Depends on her work. If she's working nights she tends to go to her own place."

Within minutes they were back at Heron House. "The good news is it's only on the third floor. Are you up for taking the stairs?"

Calladine shot Ruth a look. "I'm not done yet, Bayliss, so less of the cheek."

"I don't want to take any chances, that's all. I can do without a repeat of what happened that day. You went down like a stone. Poor Alice thought you'd karked it."

"It was merely a warning and I heeded it. I'd like you to drop it now if you don't mind. I don't enjoy being constantly reminded of my own mortality."

"Okay, subject closed."

"I meant to ask, what name are you using now that you're married, Bayliss or Ireson?" Calladine asked.

"At work I'm still Ruth Bayliss. As for the rest, I haven't decided yet."

Calladine rolled his eyes. "Still hedging your bets then. I thought you and Jake were solid once again."

"We are, but I'm taking my time with the changeover, that's all."

"Like I said, hedging your bets."

Ruth pulled up close to the main entrance of the tower block. "Right then, let's see what the Seddons have to say for themselves."

Calladine took the three flights of stairs easily with plenty of puff in reserve. "Told you, the new regime is working."

"It'll be interesting to see how long it lasts. I know you of old, and your fondness for good whisky."

Ignoring her comment, he rang the doorbell and stood back. A teenage lad opened up, glared at them, then slammed it shut in their faces.

"That's young Dean," Ruth told him.

"Volatile bugger, isn't he?" Calladine kept his finger pressed on the bell. "Come on, Dean, open this door or we'll knock it down," he shouted.

Finally they heard a woman shout from inside. "What's all the bloody noise about?"

"Open the door," Calladine called to her.

Seconds later, the door was hauled open by an angry woman. "You've no right coming here frightening our Dean. He's been on edge since his mate Noah's body was found. It's hit him hard and he can do without being bothered by the police."

The estate grapevine again. "Why? Does he have something to hide?" Calladine asked somewhat flippantly.

The woman stared at him, not sure how to answer. "No, but Noah's mum's been on the phone. She's upset, I had to calm her down and our Dean was listening. He asked me what was up and I told him."

"We have to speak to him," Ruth told her. "It's possible he can help us find who killed Noah."

"Well, he can't, he told me he's not seen him lately."

"Can we come in, Mrs Seddon?" Calladine asked wearily. "A quick word with Dean, that's all we want. I'm sure it won't take long."

Reluctantly, she stood aside to let them in. "Dean!" she shouted. "Get your arse in here, police want a word."

It was several minutes before the lad made an appearance. Tall and gangly, his hair in need of a decent cut, he stood by the sitting room door. He looked terrified. Calladine wanted to know why that was.

"It's okay, lad, we won't eat you. We're here about your mate, Noah. When did you see him last?"

Dean shook his head, his eyes on the floor.

"C'mon, lad, surely you remember? The pair of you were best friends."

"Not since he crossed Spook."

"Ricky Spooner?" Ruth asked. "What happened between them?"

The lad shrugged, his eyes never leaving the carpet. "Dunno. Didn't get on, did they?"

"Why? Didn't they like each other?" Calladine asked.

"Dunno. I reckon not."

They could go on like this all day and get nowhere. "Come on, Dean, if you won't speak to me I'll take you down to the station, see if that loosens your tongue."

"Waste of time 'cause I can't tell you anything," he shot back. "I daren't. I speak to you lot and Spook'll finish me."

"He'll do no such thing," his mother screeched. "He comes near you and he'll have me to deal with. Bad reputation or not, I'll have the lot of 'em."

"There's no need for that, Mrs Seddon. If Dean genuinely knows something and he talks to us, we'll look after him," Ruth said.

Dean glared at her. "I don't want looking after. I just want leaving alone."

21

"If you know what happened to Noah, then you must tell us," she said. "Did Spooner go after him?"

He shook his head. "No. I don't think so, not himself anyway. Spook'll be like all the rest, he wants someone fixing he'll get his thugs to sort it. He wouldn't get his own hands dirty, and even if I do speak to you, you'll never make anything stick, he's too clever."

Ruth smiled. "There is such a thing as evidence, Dean. You tell us what happened, we get witness statements, gather evidence and we put him away."

"Bollocks! That won't work with Spook. He's got money and can hire the best lawyers. Anyway it's not Spook you should look at. Lately I saw Noah hanging about with some of Barton's lot."

Now they were getting somewhere. Barton was Spook's rival. "You're saying that Noah was part of Barton's crew?"

The lad finally looked up at them, tight-lipped, and gave a nod.

"Okay." Calladine sighed. "When was the last time you saw Noah?"

"Weeks ago. He's been keeping his head down. The best thing for him if he'd thrown in his lot with Barton's mob. Spook runs the Hobfield and doesn't take kindly to folk deserting him."

"D'you have any evidence to back that up?" Ruth asked.

"Told you, I'm saying nowt."

"Noah wasn't sleeping at home, so where was he living?"

"No idea, not here — we've no room."

"Are you sure you don't recall when you saw Noah last?"

He looked at Ruth. "It were ages ago. The last time I saw him was that Saturday the kid was killed. We didn't speak, Noah was busy having an argument with one of Spook's goons."

"What kid?" Calladine asked.

"Little Alfie Lovell," Dean's mother explained. "Poor mite was mown down by a speeding car on the road that runs around the estate."

Calladine gave Ruth a questioning look. "Do we know who by?"

"No, and we suspect a car found torched on the waste ground was the one that killed him. The fire destroyed everything, forensics couldn't get anything from it, so no evidence," she said. "Flecks of dark blue and white paint were found on Alfie's clothing, thought to be from the vehicle that hit him."

"So the death was investigated?"

Ruth shook her head. This was a conversation best had in private. "There's plenty of rumours but no one's given us anything positive."

He had missed a lot, Calladine realised. He handed the lad a card. "Okay, Dean, you remember anything else or decide you want to talk to us, you'll get me on this number."

CHAPTER FIVE

"Alfie Lovell. Why do I get the impression the case has been shelved?" Calladine and Ruth were back in the car.

"It hasn't," Ruth said, "but there's not much we can do if we've no evidence and no one will speak to us."

"Same old story then. Is the hit and run down to this Spook too?"

"Might be but I doubt it. As I said, paint fragments on the boy's jeans are thought to come from a Ford. Spook drives something more pricey."

"How old was the boy?"

"Six. According to the report, he was playing football on the land at the side of Heron House with a mate when the vehicle came out of nowhere and hit him at speed."

"Does he have a family?"

"His parents are Ken and Barbara Lovell. I know them both. Ken's a self-employed painter and decorator and he's been doing some work at the centre. Babs helps out with the kids. Since her son's death she's been a regular. Alfie was their only child and she reckons it helps to keep busy."

"When was the accident?" Calladine asked.

"Not long after you were took ill."

"And there's been no hint, no word on the estate about who's responsible? Now that is odd. In cases like this we often get a tip-off."

"I agree. There are any number of villains on the Hobfield but they draw the line at sheltering hit and run drivers who kill kids. But to be fair, Tom, it might not have been down to anyone off the Hobfield. Back then, that road was something of a magnet for any boy racer in Leesworth and beyond who fancied his chances. Not anymore. The council have laid speed bumps right round and that's stopped it dead."

Calladine couldn't recall reading about the accident in the local paper and knew nothing about it. "Did you speak to the boy's friend, the one he was playing with at the time?"

"He's six, Tom, and he was traumatised. Me and Alice both spoke to him. He couldn't recall much but his mum knows to contact us if anything changes."

Calladine made a mental note to look the incident up once he was back at the station. "What d'you reckon to this Spook person? Is he a candidate for Noah's murder?"

Ruth gave a shrug. "Difficult to say but Dean's right, if Spook decided to make an example of Noah for ditching the gang, he wouldn't have done the deed himself, far too smart."

"Okay, back to the station, we'll get some lunch and decide what we've got," Calladine said.

"That won't take long. Right now we have to hope that Natasha finds something. Noah wasn't whiter than white but he wasn't as bad as some," Ruth said.

"He used to work for Spooner's mob and then switched to Barton? That's not bad?"

She shrugged. "According to Dean, but we can't take that as gospel."

"I'd like to meet Ricky Spooner and this Luke Barton. What d'you reckon?" Calladine said.

"We've got nothing on either of them, but a quick chat would do no harm."

"Once we know what the post-mortem throws up, we'll speak to Spooner first."

* * *

Ruth got herself a pack of sandwiches and a coffee from the canteen and went back up to the incident room. It was way past lunchtime and she was starving. Calladine had brought his own food and was sitting in the main office with Rocco.

"Chicken salad and fruit juice." He grimaced. "What I wouldn't give for pie and chips."

"I'm sure Kitty lets you have the odd treat now and again," Ruth said, sitting down opposite the pair.

"I'm allowed a can of low alcohol beer at night — some treat," he said.

Ruth smiled. "You know you're loving it, and without her input you'd be lost. I reckon Kitty came along just at the right time."

Calladine wasn't listening, his eyes were fixed on the computer monitor. He was busy scrolling through the cases the station had dealt with during his absence. Apart from the hit and run, there was the usual motley mixture of violence and robbery, almost all of it taking place on the Hobfield. Apart, that is, from a series of late shop break-ins that stretched all the way to Oldston. From the reports he read of that, there wasn't much evidence. No prints, no DNA and none of the shops in question had CCTV. There was a description of the lone robber though — small, thought to be young, and wearing dark clothing and a horror mask.

"I'm surprised there's been no whispers about the hit and run," Calladine said again.

"There's been nothing, Tom. Jake spoke to the kids at the centre but they all said they neither knew nor had heard anything."

"Which makes me think the culprit wasn't from the Hobfield. Like you say, a lad from elsewhere using that circular route as a racetrack."

"Greco took it up with the station at Oldston but got nowhere either. Speaking of our leader, has he welcomed you back yet?"

Calladine shot her a look. Greco wasn't his favourite person. The two men were very different. If you didn't know him, Calladine could give the impression of being disorganised and he often looked untidy. Greco, on the other hand, was as sharp as a pin mentally and fastidious about his appearance. "He rang me the Friday before I came back, asked if I was okay. I assured him I was and that was that."

"You're using that tone again and it's not fair," Ruth said. "The pair of you would get on if you gave him a chance."

A conversation about the merits of cultivating Greco as a friend wasn't what Calladine wanted right now. They were different, had different thought processes and different ways of working. Apart from which, Greco had that OCD thing and was always tidying up and picking bits up off the floor, an irritating habit Calladine couldn't abide. Time to get the team's mind back to the job in hand. "Rocco," he said. "Do we know where this Spooner person lives?"

"Lowermill, sir. With his parents in that old stone house by the Dog and Partridge pub."

Calladine looked across the table at Ruth. "We should have a word, see what he can tell us. Sooner rather than later. I don't think we should wait for the post-mortem results."

"A visit to Lowermill and then I'm calling it a day. Youth club's on tonight," she said. "If you're serious about coming, we start at seven."

Calladine checked the time. Lowermill and then home it was. He was about to get himself a coffee when he got a call from the desk sergeant downstairs.

CHAPTER SIX

"Take Rocco with you to see Spooner," Calladine told Ruth. "Someone's smashed Kitty's office window. It's not a CID matter but I'd better go and make sure she's okay." He checked the time, it was gone three in the afternoon. "I doubt I'll be back, so see you at the Community Centre later."

He needed to get going. The sarge downstairs said Kitty's voice had been shaky and she'd sounded scared. He scooped his jacket off the back of his chair and made for the door.

It took Calladine only minutes to get to Kitty's office on the High Street. When Sandy Cole, Leesdon's one and only private investigator, retired, Kitty had bought him out. When Calladine first met her, she had been working undercover on her first case in Leesdon, having just moved to the area.

As he pulled up, Calladine could see that the entire plate glass window was missing. It was already in the process of being boarded up. The window was large and would be expensive to replace. "Hope you're insured," he said, kissing Kitty's cheek. "You all right? Whatever did this didn't hit you?"

"I didn't know what it was. Suddenly there was glass everywhere. I got a right fright, I'm telling you."

"The glass will have to be ordered and cut to size," the man called over to her. "I'll be back tomorrow to fit it. The boards will keep things secure overnight."

"See, two visits, bound to be expensive," Calladine said. "Any idea why this happened? Have you upset a client? Got an irate husband on your tail?"

Kitty shook her head. "I doubt it was that calculated, Tom. I've no idea why anyone would target me. Just bad luck I reckon. A group of school kids passed by and the next thing the window caved in."

"Kids did this?" He was surprised. According to the reports he'd read there'd been a deal of criminal activity in the town while he'd been gone, but no wanton vandalism. Calladine wanted to question her further but Kitty looked pale. The incident had obviously upset her. "You lock up and we'll get off home. You're shaken up."

"I'll have to sort this mess first."

The office was in a state and with broken glass strewn across the floor and surfaces, dangerous. There was no way she could open up tomorrow with the place like this. Calladine knew from experience that there was no point arguing with her. Kitty had had a fright but she was a strong woman. "Okay, I'll give you a hand."

"No need," she insisted. "It's a small space and I'll do better on my own. I appreciate you dashing round and I admit for a while I was shocked, but I'm not too bad now. I just want to get the glass swept up. It'd really help if you went home and made something for us to eat later."

Fair enough, if that's what she wanted he'd make himself scarce. But he'd no intention of going home before he'd had a word with the neighbouring businesses, find out if anyone had seen what happened.

Across the road from Kitty's office was a cafe. He knew Mary, the woman who ran it. He also knew she had a CCTV camera fitted above her door that pointed into the street.

She poured Calladine a mug of tea. "Gave me a bloody shock, that did. Is Kitty okay? At first I thought she was the target but his aim was all wrong."

His? "This was the kids?" he asked.

"Kids?" Mary said. "No, I'm talking about the bloke with the rifle."

Calladine could barely believe what he was hearing. "Are you telling me that someone took a pot shot at Kitty?"

"I'm not sure he was actually aiming at her, like I said the angle was wrong. I saw the whole thing, brazen he was, didn't give a damn who witnessed what he was up to. He pulled up in a van right outside my window. He knew I was watching him because he gave me a wave, cheeky bugger. He took the gun off the passenger seat and aimed it at Kitty's office window. When I saw that, I picked up the phone and rang you lot."

"Did you get a good look at him?"

"He had one of those balaclavas on. So no, I've no idea who he was. It all seemed to happen in slow motion but I knew there was something wrong, his aim was too high. One shot rang out, the window shattered and he drove off. If he hadn't been such a good shot, heaven knows what might have happened."

Not what Kitty told him. Why would she lie? Could she have been mistaken? Saw the kids and thought it was down to them? "I'll need the footage from your camera," he told Mary.

She handed him the tea. "I'll put it on a stick. Pop in before you go home and you can take it with you."

"You sure it was a gun you saw?"

She fixed her eyes on him. "Do I look stupid, Tom? I know a rifle when I see one. He drove a dark blue transit type van and I'd say from the way he carried himself and his clothes that he were young."

"Did you recognise the van? Have you seen it around?"

"Not especially, it were just a van. There are loads of them up and down here every day."

Calladine swigged the rest of his tea, thanked her and returned to Kitty's office. This wasn't right. Kitty was hiding something and he wanted to know what. Shots fired in broad daylight in Leesdon centre, what the hell was going on?

* * *

Kitty didn't look too pleased to see him back. "I told you to go home and sort something to eat."

"I've been talking to Mary across the road." He watched Kitty stiffen. "She saw it all. The van, the young man driving it and the gun he fired at your window."

There was an awkward silence, then Kitty threw the sweeping brush to the floor, folded her arms and turned her back on him. "Leave it, Tom, please."

"I don't understand. What's going on?"

"Nothing, it's obviously a mistake."

She was lying and not convincingly. Calladine had no idea why but there was something very wrong.

"Are you being threatened, Kitty? You can tell me, I'm in a position to help you."

"I don't want you involved, Tom, so leave it."

"I can't do that," he said firmly. "A shotgun was fired at your office window in broad daylight. The bullet could have hit you, it could have hit anyone in the line of sight. The entire incident was witnessed." He shook his head. "Whether you like it or not it'll have to be investigated, and it would help if you simply told me what was going on."

"Please, Tom. I don't want you mixed up in this."

"I'm a policeman. I can't simply turn my back and pretend it never happened. Speak to me and I'll get it sorted."

"It'll have been a mistake, crossed wires. I can sort it without your help," she said.

Calladine doubted that. Kitty wasn't helping herself by staying silent. If she wouldn't tell him what this was about he'd just have to find out for himself.

"I don't want you reporting this, Tom, d'you understand?"

"I don't have much choice. It has to be checked out."

"I can't do with you lot tramping all over the place, questioning the neighbours. I'd much rather just leave it," she said.

This wasn't right. It didn't sound much like the Kitty he knew either. But the look on her face plainly said she was worried and he didn't want to upset her further. He'd have to be discreet, make his own enquiries first, before passing it forward.

"You ready for the off then?" he asked. "I've arranged to meet Ruth later at the Community Centre."

"I've still got a lot to do. You go home, I'll see you when you get back from the centre."

If that's what she wanted. "Any further trouble, you ring me. Got it?"

CHAPTER SEVEN

Large and stone built, the Spooners' home stood in its own grounds, rising tall and gaunt, casting dark shadows over the garden of the nearby Dog and Partridge pub. Rocco and Ruth strolled up the drive.

"That little lot says money to me," Rocco commented.

"His parents have a car sales business with branches all over Greater Manchester, plus interests elsewhere. Officially Ricky works at the showroom in Oldston," Ruth said.

Rocco laughed. "Wonder how many hours he puts in there of your average week? Some people — they've no idea how lucky they are."

"You sound pissed off. All not well in Rocco's world?" Ruth asked, glancing at him.

"Alice wants us to get our own place. The problem is money, pure and simple. Neither of us have wealthy parents prepared to give us a handout."

"It's serious then?" Ruth asked.

"Keep it under wraps. The boss has known for a while and he's not said owt. But you know as well as I do what he'd do if he found out."

Ruth laughed. "By 'boss', you mean Greco — who got a detective constable on his team pregnant."

"Yeah, but he married her, and Grace no longer works in the force. I'm not sure Alice is ready for that," Rocco said.

Ruth rang the bell, which was answered by a middle-aged woman. Rocco showed her his badge and asked for Ricky Spooner.

"He's not here. His mother needed his help in the office today."

"Is that the showroom in Oldston?" Rocco asked.

"Yes." She glared at Rocco. "But don't go bothering him there. They've got the monthly accounts to do. Neither of them will thank you for disturbing the day's work."

Ruth handed her a card. "Tell Ricky we called and give him that. If he gives me a ring, I'll make arrangements to see him." She turned and led the way back down the drive.

"Is that it?" Rocco asked. "We just leave it there?"

"We don't have anything on Ricky Spooner, other than hearsay and gut feeling. Before we go back to the nick we'll give Luke Barton a visit, weigh him up, ask what he's been up to."

"Where does he live?" Rocco asked.

Ruth smiled. "Guess. Where do all the up and coming villains — apart from this one — live?"

"Back to the Hobfield it is then."

* * *

Luke Barton lived with his mother and two younger siblings in the same row of houses as Noah Crosby. Ruth banged on the front door, to be confronted by an elderly woman. She looked angry.

"You here about the attack on Luke?"

Ruth shook her head. "No. Is he okay? What happened to him?"

"There's been some sort of incident near those bloody towers, and my Luke's ended up in hospital," the woman said.

"Is he badly hurt?" Ruth asked.

"He was set upon by a madman with a knife. The hospital rang and his mum dashed out of here like the devil himself was after her."

"And you are?"

"Martha Barton, his granny, I live round the corner. What d'you want? I can't hang about here. I'm worried sick, the minute the younger ones get home from school I'm off to the hospital myself. I need to know how he is. That boy means the world to me, I practically raised him."

"Leesdon General?" Rocco asked. Martha nodded.

"D'you know when he was assaulted?" Ruth asked.

"About an hour ago. But why anyone would take a knife to him is a mystery to me."

Ruth could take a pretty good guess. He was suspected of dealing, and if that was right, he must know plenty of users. Refuse to supply a desperate customer and it could get you hurt.

"Hopefully he's well enough to tell us who attacked him," Rocco said.

"I hope so," Martha said. "And when he does, you lot make sure you throw the book at them."

They went back to the car. Ruth handed Rocco the keys. "Leesdon General and then I'm calling it a day."

Rocco nodded. "It'll be a falling out over drugs. With luck we might get something on him this time."

Ruth checked the time on her mobile and then called Jake. "I'm going to be late, so it'll mean you or Babs opening up the centre. And Tom says he'll drop in. No fuss, just let him mingle and watch what goes on."

"I hope you warned him not to push the copper thing. The kids are wary enough of you without that."

"He'll be fine, you worry too much. You okay to get things ready?"

"No problem, Babs is already hard at it. Her and Trudy have been there most of the afternoon organising the costumes for the play."

"Brilliant. See you when I can." Ruth popped her mobile in her pocket and leaned back in the seat. She'd forgotten Trudy was giving Babs a hand today, given the circumstances her help was most welcome.

The youth club had a theatre group and they planned to put on a performance later in the year. Trudy had contacts with a group of players attached to the church and had borrowed a number of costumes.

"Wonder who it was that had a go at Barton," Rocco said.

"On the Hobfield? Could have been anyone — a user, or another dealer he supplied. I've never met him, but those who have say he's easy to dislike, full of his own self-importance."

"What does he do for a living — apart from dealing, that is?"

"He works at Goddard's garden centre. And there's no evidence of him dealing remember, it's only a suspicion," Ruth said.

"Bet it's on the nail though, given he's Hobfield born and bred."

* * *

Twenty minutes later the pair pulled into the hospital car park. Rocco asked the receptionist where Barton was, and they were directed to the relatives' room, where the young man's mother and a uniformed officer were waiting.

"How is he?" Rocco asked.

"Half dead," Irene Barton said hysterically. "He was stabbed and he's lost a lot of blood. I want the bastard who did this catching, d'you hear me? My son's set upon and knifed in broad daylight. No one sees anything or hears his screams for help. What is wrong with the people on that estate?"

"Have you any idea what Luke was doing there? Shouldn't he have been at work?" Ruth asked.

"How should I know? I don't keep tabs on his every move."

"Has he said anything about the attack since he was found and brought in?" Ruth asked the uniform.

Irene Barton gave Ruth a filthy look. "Like who did this to him, you mean. That would make your job easy, wouldn't it? But no, he didn't. My son has been assaulted. When I heard I panicked, imagined all sorts." She began to sob. "Just make sure someone pays, because I will be on your backs until they're up in court."

Ruth wanted a word with the doctor treating him, find out for herself just how bad Barton was. She nodded to Rocco. "Stay with her, I won't be long."

Ruth went to the emergency department reception, hoping to find a medic who'd talk to her. The receptionist was no help, she didn't even bother to speak, pointing instead to an empty chair in the crowded room. Ruth had no idea how long this would take. The place was busy, that meant the staff were working flat out. She was about to return to Rocco when across the room she spotted an old friend, Dr Sebastian Hoyle. He now worked at the hospital part-time, but prior to retiring he'd had Natasha Barrington's job as Leesworth's pathologist.

Hurrying to his side, she tapped his shoulder. "Shouldn't you have your feet up somewhere, Doc?"

He greeted her with a broad grin. "Ruth, how nice to see you. Is Tom here too?"

"No, and this isn't a social call, I'm afraid. I'm interested in a young man brought in this afternoon. A stabbing victim, one Luke Barton."

Doc Hoyle nodded and beckoned for her to follow him, pointing to a cubicle. "That's him in there with his arm in a sling, looking decidedly sorry for himself."

Barton was tall with blond hair, dressed from head to toe in designer sports gear, although the hoodie he wore had a lot of blood on it. "Is it okay if I have a quick word?"

"Go ahead, he's not that delicate."

Ruth entered the cubicle, introduced herself and smiled at him. "Want to tell me what happened, Luke?"

"No need, I won't be pressing charges anyway." He returned her smile.

"That's not the point. We can't have people assaulted and stabbed and not do something about it. Besides your mum is upset and she's itching to throw the book at someone."

"I was set upon, Sergeant. I don't know who by, I didn't see his face. Fortunately, I've got excellent reflexes, hence the flesh wound and not something more serious."

"He got your arm?" she asked.

"Yes, but I'll mend."

"You're sure you've no idea why you were assaulted? Was it a robbery?" Ruth asked.

"If it was, he didn't get anything. He came at me from behind but I managed to spin round. That's when he got my arm."

At that moment a doctor entered the cubicle. "The X-ray is fine. A nurse at your own GP clinic will take the stitches out in five days. When you're ready, you can go home."

Barton turned to Ruth. "See? It's no biggy, just another fracas on that damned estate."

"That damned estate you happen to live on. Sure you don't want to tell me what happened? They could try again, and anyway, why didn't any of your friends jump in to help you?"

"I was alone, on my way back to work. I'd nipped home to have some dinner."

"Sure you didn't recognise your attacker?" Ruth asked.

"No, he wore a balaclava. Obviously someone who fancied his chances. The gear I'm wearing, it's expensive, gives the wrong impression. People see it and think I've got money. An attempted mugging gone wrong, I'd say."

Ruth gave him one of her unimpressed looks. She didn't believe a word of it. "I'd be more careful in future if I was you." She handed him a card. "You were friendly with Noah Crosby, weren't you? You'll have heard he was killed."

"Shame, he was an all right kid. Useful, happy to run errands, but that was the extent of our friendship, Sergeant. Noah was too volatile for me, always in trouble."

Ruth didn't believe that either, but she needed more information before facing him with the truth. "If anything occurs to you, if you do recall who did this, ring me."

Ruth waited until Barton was in the corridor out of earshot and then collared the doctor who'd treated him. "Did he have anything on him when he was brought in?"

"Not by the time he got to me. He came in an ambulance so the paramedics might know."

Ruth collected Rocco and they went down to the hospital reception to asked if the paramedics were still there. She was in luck, the pair were in the canteen getting something to eat.

The senior one, a man called Neil, couldn't be sure but his partner, Lisa, nodded. "There was something. We found him on the ground near the tower blocks clutching a carrier bag. Whoever knifed him was long gone. His arm was bleeding heavily and needing treating but he wasn't parting with the bag."

"Important then," Ruth said. "What happened to the bag?"

"Despite the pain he was in, he chucks the bag to one of a group of lads standing round ogling us. I'm surprised he had the strength to be honest. Whatever it was, I'd say it was very important."

CHAPTER EIGHT

Calladine still lived in the street he'd been born in, the street where his late mother, and her mother before her, had lived all their lives. When he left home, he simply followed suit, bought a terraced cottage a few doors down and had not moved since.

Over the years he'd had a number of women living with him, but none of them had become permanent. Kitty was one more in a long line, as Ruth had been keen to point out. But he liked her and had hopes that their romance might stay the course. However, as he was coming to realise, Kitty valued her independence and insisted on keeping the flat above her office as her home. Until he knew more about why someone had shot at her office window, he'd do his best to persuade her to stay with him.

He didn't have long, just an hour or so before he had to be at the centre. Time for a quick bite and to feed Sam, his dog. The animal was old and set in his ways, a lot like him. When Calladine entered the small living room, Sam gave him a quick glance, yawned and then went back to sleep on the sofa. A neighbour, Ryan, a young lad from across the road, walked Sam for Calladine when he was at work, which meant the dog had had his exercise for the day. "Don't worry, fella,

I won't disturb you." He wrote a short note for Kitty and left it on the coffee table.

He'd meant to spruce the place up while he'd been off but hadn't got round to it. The living room could do with a lick of paint for starters. Kitty thought the place old fashioned and dark. A case in point was the large mahogany sideboard against one wall that had belonged to his grandmother. If he was serious about persuading Kitty to move in, he'd have to do something about modernising the place.

Before he went out again he wanted a look at the memory stick Mary had given him. He stuck it in his laptop and found the footage. She was right, the bloke didn't seem to care who saw him. But then he did have a balaclava on and appeared to be well practised at what he was doing. The whole operation took only seconds. He pulled up, took hold of the rifle, fired the shot and was gone. Blink and you'd have missed it. Whoever he was, he was no amateur. And that made Calladine nervous.

* * *

A mug of coffee, a change of clothes and he was on the move again. No need to take the car, the Hobfield wasn't far away and the walk would do him good. As he approached the estate he could see a group of kids gathered at the entrance to the centre. No sign of Ruth's car but Jake's pedal bike was chained up outside. He also spotted a taped off area with a uniformed officer on watch. He wanted to go and ask what had gone on but decided against it. The kids would notice and it would just reinforce his identity as a copper.

The main hall was a large, busy space with plenty of youngsters milling about. A number of trestle tables were positioned around the perimeter, piled high with clothing.

A woman he didn't know walked towards him. "Babs Lovell," she said. "You must be Tom, Ruth's friend."

Calladine smiled back and nodded. He recognised the name. This was the woman who'd lost her son in the hit

41

and run. He debated with himself for a few moments as to whether to say something, but what? For now he decided against it. The woman would still be grieving.

"Ruth not here yet?" he asked.

"No, but Jake's over there."

Babs Lovell was young, no more than thirty, and painfully thin. She had short dark hair that she kept fiddling with. As she spoke to Calladine her eyes were constantly darting around the room. Was she simply keeping tabs on the kids, he wondered, or was she the nervous type?

"We're putting together costumes for the play we hope to put on later in the year," she said.

"Want me to get stuck in?"

"You can help Killian over there. He's trying, without much luck, to put together an outfit for a soldier."

The lad was flushed, rummaging impatiently through a pile of jackets and hats. Calladine went over to join him. "Hi, Killian. Need a hand?"

The lad scowled back at him. "What d'you want now?"

"Nothing," Calladine said. "I'm here to help out. Jake over there is a friend of mine."

Killian Seddon didn't look convinced. "You're a copper, you lot always want something."

Ignoring the comment, Calladine held up an old RAF jacket. "It's not army but we could use this."

Killian snatched the garment from Calladine and threw it onto a chair with some boots. "What do I call you?"

"Tom." Calladine smiled. "There's drinks over there on the table, want one?"

Killian nodded warily. "Get me a coke and a slice of that chocolate cake."

Calladine disappeared, returning shortly with two bottles of coke and two chocolate brownies. "They do a nice spread, cheap too." He handed the lad his. "Your Dean not come here then?"

"See, knew you were fishing."

"He might like it. There's plenty of kids his age to mix with. Better to be in here with your mates having a good time than out on the streets."

Killian grunted. "Dean's got other ideas about having a good time."

"Is he feeling any better? He was in a right state this afternoon. For such a young lad he seems to have the woes of the world on his shoulders. Your mum must worry about how he gets."

"Dean's an idiot, needs to stop messing with trouble," Killian said.

Calladine rummaged through the clothing, yanked out a military looking cap and handed it to the lad. "A badge or two on this and it'll look the business. By trouble you mean Spooner, I suppose?"

Killian glared at Calladine and gave him a shove. "Go and bother someone else. I don't know what's up with Dean and I don't care, but he needs to watch it. Spook might be a fucking moron but he's not the problem. My brother crosses the wrong person, like Noah did, and he'll go the same way."

"You don't think Spook did for Noah? Got any other names?" Calladine asked.

"Even if I had, I wouldn't tell you. I don't want to end up one dark night with a knife in my back."

"You surprise me, Killian. I thought the estate was terrified of Spook. I'd no idea there was someone even more dangerous out there."

"I don't know anything, just what I hear. *He's* back, that's what my mum thinks anyway. She says it's been years but men like him don't change."

Now Calladine was really interested. "Men like what? Want to tell me more?"

"No, now shove off."

"Tom!" It was Ruth calling to him. "You got here then. What d'you think?"

Calladine went over to stand with her. He took a long look round the space. "You and Jake have done well. This lot seem to be having a good time and they're off the streets, which is no bad thing. Did you learn anything from Barton?"

Ruth groaned. "You don't know, do you? Sorry, it's been manic since earlier and I haven't had a minute to catch up. Barton was attacked, knifed here on the Hobfield this afternoon. Lucky for him it's not serious. A few stitches and he was able to go home."

That solved the problem of the taped off area outside. "Any witnesses? Anyone see what happened?"

Ruth snorted. "What d'you think? I had uniform ask around but no one saw anything, heard anything, or can help in any way. We've got the usual big fat nothing from everyone, and Barton's not saying a word. But he did have the strength left to chuck a carrier bag at a friend before he was carted off. No idea what was in it though. The paramedics who attended were too intent on stemming the bleeding."

Calladine sighed. "As if we didn't have enough to think about."

"It might be connected to Noah's death. That's now big news all over the town so perhaps someone is getting nervy," Ruth said.

"Could be, but who? Spooner? Barton? Killian over there tells me his mum thinks it's someone from the past but then he clammed up. We've got no chance of finding out if folk won't talk to us. And as if this little lot wasn't enough, someone took a pot shot at Kitty's office window this afternoon."

Ruth's eyes widened. "They fired a gun, in the middle of town? Is she okay?"

"She reckons so, but she's hiding something. I think Kitty knows very well who's behind it but she's another one who won't talk," Calladine said.

Just then, a man came up behind them. "Have either of you seen Babs?"

Ruth smiled at him. "Ken, glad you could come. Yes, she's over there, helping sort the costumes. You okay?"

44

"Got to be, haven't I. I've got work on. Take too much time off and my customers will go elsewhere."

"I think I told you, Ken's a self-employed painter and decorator," Ruth said to Calladine.

He nodded. That could be handy. "You taking on jobs at the moment? Only I could do with my sitting room sprucing up."

"Need all the work I can get," Ken said, "but you'll have to give me a couple of days to finish the current job."

Calladine smiled. "Fine by me. Want to come and take a look, let me see a couple of colour charts or whatever?"

"Tomorrow evening suit?"

Calladine nodded, scribbled his home address on one of his cards and handed it to him. "Thanks. See you tomorrow then."

"What're you up to?" Ruth asked, watching Ken wander away.

"I do the place up, let Kitty choose the colour scheme and she might be more inclined to move in properly. I don't have the time and I'm no decorator."

"You reckon the way to a woman's heart is through a fancy roll of wallpaper," she scoffed. "You've got a lot to learn, Tom Calladine."

CHAPTER NINE

Wednesday

The following morning Calladine and Ruth were due to go to the Duggan Centre. Neither was looking forward to the post-mortem, and given the state of Noah's body, neither envied Natasha her task.

"Reckon we'll get much?" Ruth asked.

"Difficult to judge, given the state of him. His phone is the best bet. Finding out who he last spoke to for instance," Calladine said.

"I've left Alice with that one. Comms are working as fast as they can. The minute the report's through, we'll be told," Ruth said. "Enjoy yourself last night?"

Calladine pulled a face. "The kids don't say much. Apart from that snippet Killian told me about his mother's theory, he was decidedly guarded. I'd say someone was putting pressure on him to keep his mouth shut."

"What theory?"

"That someone is back and up to his old tricks. At least that's what he said. No names, mind you, and that was all I got."

"I've tried asking him about Noah, Tom, but got nowhere. All the kids are jumpy. Some genuinely have no idea what's going on but they know enough to keep silent. It's been that way for a while. Jake found one of his pupils, young Billy Knowles, in tears last week. All he'd say to explain himself was that his family might have to move. Jake got the impression they were being intimidated in some way. Billy ducked out of a trip they were going on because his dad had told him they might not be living here for much longer."

"The kid could have got things mixed up. Overheard half a conversation at home," Calladine said.

"Jake didn't think so. He asked him about it and it was then Billy burst into tears. Said his mum has told him not to answer the door and won't let him out on his own. That smacks of them being threatened to me."

"Do we know them?" Calladine asked.

"His dad is Rob Knowles, he's a market trader. He runs a stall on the Oldston market twice a week as well as the one in Lowermill. They're a nice family, don't cause any trouble. Billy's only twelve."

"And Jake has no more details?" Calladine asked.

"The lad won't say much, but it seems something happened at his dad's lock-up. Jake only got that much because he spoke to one of Billy's pals."

"Is it local, this lock-up?" Calladine asked.

"Back of the library, one of those new units. Ken Lovell has one too, uses it to store his stock and equipment," Ruth said.

Calladine nodded. "We could take a wander that way later, speak to all the businesses with units there, see what we can glean."

"Is Kitty okay this morning?" Ruth asked. "What happened must have been a right shock."

"And not just for her," he said. "Problem is, she won't discuss it. I can only presume it's connected to a case she's working on, but if she's up against some individual happy to fire off a rifle in the centre of town she's on a loser. Wish she'd let me in. I might be able to help. Instead she's trying to pretend it never happened, but I've seen the CCTV footage.

I watched him pull up, grab the rifle and take the shot, no hesitation."

"Do you know him?"

"He wore a balaclava and was in black clothing, so I've no idea."

Ruth had a quick glimpse at her notes from the day before. "Barton said that his attacker wore a balaclava. What d'you think, same man?"

"Could be but what self-respecting villain doesn't wear one when out on the rampage?" Calladine said drily.

"You need to get Kitty to talk to you," Ruth said.

"She will before long, she's a sensible woman," Calladine said. "Let's just hope nothing else happens in the meantime. Anyway, I've no intention of letting it drop. I can't — a rifle fired in the High Street in broad daylight. Whether Kitty likes it or not it'll have to be investigated."

"Killian reckons you're okay. Said he was surprised you were so '*normal*'." Ruth chuckled. "Mind you, he doesn't know you like I do."

"He didn't give me that impression," Calladine said.

"It's just his way. I hope you intend to come back. Killian's put both your and Ken's names down for scenery painting next week. We're starting rehearsals too, and there're a lot of lines to learn."

Calladine made a face. "I'm not much good at that sort of thing."

"At a pinch we could even find you a part. What d'you think?"

He smiled. "I think you're joking. Did you get any intel on Spooner?"

"Not a word. The kids are scared. No one talks about Spooner as a rule. What happened yesterday with Barton has upset the equilibrium of the estate."

"That estate doesn't have any equilibrium," Calladine scoffed. "It's a bloody mess, lurches from one catastrophe to another."

"You'll get more out of the kids once they learn to trust you. Join us again next week, help Killian and the others with the painting. You might learn something from their chat," she said.

Calladine had his doubts that they'd say anything in front of him. Mistrust was ingrained in Hobfield residents from birth. "Painting scenery, eh. He's got a lot of faith in me. I can't even paint my own walls. I'm getting that bloke in, remember."

"Ken'll do a good job," she said.

"Tricky though. What do I say to him after what happened to his son? I read through the report and we weren't much help. No one's been brought to book and we've got no suspects. He can't be happy with how things have been left."

"Ken doesn't think like that. He knows we tried our best and what we're up against. He also knows that we haven't stopped looking for the driver."

"Where does he live, this Ken?" Calladine asked.

"The road at the back of me, in one of the bungalows."

Calladine considered this. It was a good ten-minute walk from Ruth's house to the estate. "What was the child doing on the Hobfield? Surely he hadn't wandered there on his own?"

"The boys had arranged to play football that afternoon. His best pal lives on the estate. The kids weren't doing any harm, just playing on the spare ground opposite the towers. The car came out of nowhere, hit Alfie and roared off. The other boys ran away, apart from his pal, and he can't remember what happened accurately enough. Alfie was hit hard, tossed into the air, and landed heavily on concrete. His pal was rightly traumatised by what he witnessed."

"Poor little sod. A case of wrong place, wrong time," Calladine said.

CHAPTER TEN

In the morgue, Noah Crosby was laid out on a table. He looked even worse than when Calladine had first seen him in the alley. Lying naked with his flesh eaten away and rotting, the spectacle wasn't helped by the vicious looking wound to his neck. It was horrific, and the smell wasn't much better.

"I don't know how you do this job," he said to Natasha, clamping a mask to his face.

"Someone has to, Tom," she said.

Calladine pointed a gloved finger at Crosby's throat. "How long since he got that?"

"The best I can do is about three to four weeks. We can study the insect life further, but it's a reasonable estimate," she said.

"We have his mobile, that might give us a better timescale."

Dreadful as it was, Calladine's gaze was drawn back to the body. Noah's neck wound was hideous, it stretched from one ear to the other. "It's deep too," Natasha confirmed. "Cut both the carotid artery and oesophagus in two. I'd say it was made by one of those large straight-edged kitchen knives."

"The killer definitely wanted him dead then," Calladine said.

Natasha had Noah rolled over. "There is also this." She pointed to a mark on his back.

"Another stab wound?" Ruth asked.

"Yes, but this one wouldn't have been fatal. It would have stopped him in his tracks though."

"So, someone came up behind him and did that," Calladine said. "Realising it wasn't enough, they cut his throat."

"Well, that's for you to decide but from a pathologist's point of view, it looks that way." She pointed to his legs. "It's difficult to see with the decomposition, but there are marks on both knees that look like bruises. That suggests he was stabbed in the back, fell hard onto his knees and then the fatal wound was delivered."

"Are there any other injuries? Had he been beaten first?" Ruth asked.

"The state of the body makes that difficult to assess but the X-ray shows no broken bones."

Calladine shook his head. What had Noah done to end up like this? He'd upset someone big style, that was for sure.

Natasha pointed to Noah's back. She handed him a magnifying glass. "And then there's this."

Due to the state of the body, Calladine wasn't sure what he was looking at.

"It's hard to spot but look, it's a distinct letter 'X' and it's been carved into the flesh."

The sight sparked a distant memory, a horrific one. Calladine felt suddenly queasy. This was something he'd never expected to see again. "That mark wasn't got by accident, it's too precisely done."

Natasha agreed. "You've gone pale. Have you seen this before?"

Calladine nodded. "A long time ago. It was the handiwork of a killer who stalked the Hobfield for weeks. Despite throwing a shed load of resources at the case, we never caught him. Each of his victims had their throat cut and had that same initial carved somewhere on their skin."

This piqued Ruth's interest. "Didn't you have any idea who he or she was?"

"It was definitely a male, he spoke to one of his victims and was overheard by a witness hiding nearby, but that's all we know," Calladine said.

"How long ago was this?" Ruth asked.

"I'll have to check, but it must have been twenty, twenty-five years ago. Back then we named him 'the Shadow' because we had no name for him, and all the witnesses who came forward said that's all they saw, a dark shadow in the moonlight."

"Did he always attack in the dark?" Ruth asked.

Calladine nodded.

"But he can't be back, surely?" Ruth said, puzzled. "It's too long ago, and why the gap?"

"Perhaps it's someone who's read about the case," Natasha suggested.

"Sounds feasible," Ruth said.

"Except for one important fact," Calladine said. "The bit about the carving on the body was never released to the press. No one who wasn't involved with the case knew about it."

Ruth stared at him. "What're you saying?"

"Exactly that. I have no explanation for what's happening, I'm just relating the facts." Calladine shook himself. To be faced with this after such a long time had upset him. "Noah Crosby is the first victim in years. If this is down to the same killer, we've got a problem."

"Perhaps he was apprehended for something else and went inside," Ruth suggested. "Or simply moved away. For all we know he's been committing this sort of crime elsewhere in the county."

It was a mystery, and it made Calladine uneasy. "You can run a check when we get back to the nick." He looked at Natasha. "Is Julian around?"

Natasha nodded towards his office. "He's asked to have a word while you're here."

Professor Julian Batho was the senior forensic scientist at the Duggan and an old friend of the pair. But where Calladine was concerned, Julian was more than that. He was the biological father of his granddaughter, Maisie.

He nudged Ruth. "Let's see what he's got."

* * *

Julian Batho never looked particularly happy. He was an intense man, someone who took his work seriously and rarely cracked a joke. The detectives entered his lab to find him standing at his bench, staring into a microscope. He looked up momentarily, frowned and beckoned them over.

"Noah Crosby. I've been studying the clothing he was found in."

"Bet that was fun," said Calladine drily.

Taller than Calladine, Julian looked down his long nose at Calladine. "It's no joking matter, Tom."

"I'm not joking, Julian. He'd been decomposing for weeks."

"There's precious little to be gained from the body. Toxicology, such as it is, gave us nothing, save that he wasn't an addict, which surprised me given where he came from." Julian pointed to the microscope.

Calladine took a look but was none the wiser. "What am I looking at?"

"Flour, and a lot of it. It was all over his jeans, on his hoodie and even in his hair."

"The flour you bake with?" Calladine asked. "What on earth had he been doing?"

Julian shrugged. "It's odd, I agree, certainly not what I would have expected to find."

"Anything else useful?" Calladine asked.

Julian looked him up and down. He shook his head. "He'd been dead a while, and the maggots had done plenty of damage. There was a deal of grit and earth on his jeans, possibly from when he was attacked. It matches the soil on the land in front of the towers."

Calladine nodded. "Killed on the Hobfield and dumped in that alley. Poor sod."

"His trainers are interesting too," Julian said. "They're high end and I mean high — the really expensive sort. Where does a young lad off the Hobfield get the money from to buy shoes like that?"

Ruth smiled. "Didn't have you down as an expert on trainers, Julian."

"I'm not, but I did a little research. This brand doesn't sell anything under the five hundred mark. I've seen the advertising for similar and the price tags are eye-watering. I thought the information might prove important somewhere down the line."

"Wonder where Noah got them from and how he afforded them?" Ruth mused.

"Where he'd been that night to end up covered in flour and knifed to death is more to the point," Calladine said. "His mum's place is on the other side of the estate."

"According to her, he was rarely ever there," Ruth said. "He had to have been bedding down with a mate somewhere. There are a couple of flats on the ground floor of Heron House that aren't officially occupied. The homeless use them at times, perhaps Noah did too."

Calladine smiled at Julian. "Thanks. What you've found is a start. Where it takes us is anyone's guess."

"Amy's arriving any day," Julian said quickly, gave a nervous cough and immediately returned to his microscope.

He meant his aunt Amy who, apart from Maisie, was his only living relative. Given that Julian had no parents, Amy saw herself as Maisie's granny.

"Is she staying long?" Calladine asked.

Julian waited several seconds before replying. Finally, he said, "She wants to move back. She loves Cornwall but all the family she has left is here."

Calladine supposed he should be pleased for his friend, but Amy Dean and him had history. There had been a time when he'd thought they had a future, but Amy had ended the romance by moving to Cornwall. He had been upset at the time. Now she was moving back because of Maisie, and that meant she'd feature prominently in his life too. Calladine wasn't sure how he felt about that.

"Will she open her business again?" Amy had been running a 'new age' shop when she and Calladine first met. Apart from the weird and wonderful stuff she sold in the shop, she read Tarot cards and went by the name 'Amaris'.

"Amy's never stopped working. She does readings online these days, but she has expressed an interest in starting up again."

Calladine nodded. "Folk still ask me about her."

"Zoe has agreed to let me have Maisie on Sunday afternoon. Me and Amy will take her for a walk around the park and along by the canal."

Calladine grunted. "Lucky you. It's more than she allows me. I can only take the infant out in her pram if either Zoe or Jo come with me. Makes me feel like some incompetent oldie."

"I am Maisie's father and you've not been well, Tom," Julian reminded him. "Zoe is just being her usual sensible self."

"Well, I wish she'd cut me some slack. Remember, I'm her dad. I'm also a member of this family and a responsible adult. If there was any chance of me keeling over again, I'd say so."

Julian gave him a rare smile. "Zoe's doing a great job. Motherhood suits her, Jo too, and Maisie is thriving."

"Glad you approve," Calladine said. "No doubt I'll see Amy during her visit, catch up on the news."

"I know she'd like that. Amy is still fond of you, you know."

Ignoring the comment, Calladine asked, "Will she be looking for somewhere to live during her visit, make plans for the move?"

"Jo has already sent her some information about properties for sale," Julian said.

Jo Brandon, Zoe's partner, was an estate agent. She and Zoe had premises on the High Street in Lowermill. Jo had the ground floor and Zoe, who was a solicitor, had offices on the first.

"You know what she's like, Tom. She'll weigh things up and go from there. But I do know she's sold her place in Cornwall, so she's ready to go."

CHAPTER ELEVEN

As soon as they returned from the Duggan, Calladine pulled out the old notes from the Shadow case and then gathered the team together in the incident room. Rocco and Alice sat together at the back, whispering and swapping meaningful looks. He smiled to himself — so the romance was still going strong. Ruth was busy filling the board with what they had so far, and a handful of uniformed officers lurked at the rear of the room.

Calladine nodded to one of them. "Close the door. What I have to say is for this team only."

This started a general mumble of anticipation around the room. "Noah Crosby," Calladine began. "Stabbed and left to rot in an alley on the Hobfield. He might still be there if it wasn't for the warm weather." He cleared his throat. This was a very real possibility and horrific to contemplate. "Forensic evidence suggests he met his end on the rough ground in front of the towers. As is usual with the Hobfield, no one is saying much except that he may have had a falling out with one Ricky Spooner, aka Spook, and migrated to Luke Barton's mob. Now, Barton too was knifed yesterday. His quick reflexes meant he was able to fend off the assailant but he maintains he's no idea who it was."

"Retaliation for Noah?" Rocco suggested.

"Possibly. Talk on the estate strongly suggests there are two factions embroiled in a gang war, each trying to take the Hobfield for themselves. One faction is led by Ricky Spooner and the other by Luke Barton."

Alice put her hand up. "I've done some research, sir."

Calladine nodded for her to continue.

"Spooner comes from a well-heeled family and went to private school then Manchester University. Barton, on the other hand, was dragged up on the Hobfield by his single mother. She left him with his grandmother when he was four and didn't return until he was twelve. Since then the three of them have lived at the same address.

"Despite Spooner's education he hasn't done anything special jobwise. He works in the family car sales business and does appear to put the hours in. Barton, on the other hand, has had a variety of jobs. Currently he works as a labourer at Goddard's garden centre, a job he's had off and on since leaving school. But he has done other things, he worked on the bins for a while and did a stint at Northern Sportswear, although he only lasted a week there. On paper they both look fine, particularly Spooner. Neither has a police record."

"So why all the rumours about dealing drugs, particularly around Spooner? The world and his wife has that young man down as a bad 'un," Ruth said. "Okay, on paper they both might be fine but we've got one death and one wounding, and that is down to someone. We all know the Hobfield and what goes on there. What's happening has to be down to drugs and two gangs vying for control. Something else. Whoever went for Barton with a knife wore a balaclava, just like the man involved in that other incident you mentioned, sir."

Calladine noticed the interested looks. Ruth was talking about Kitty but he wasn't ready to go official on that yet. "We need more than suspicion and rumour," he said. "But I agree, experience tells us this is more than likely drug-related."

"Before he was carted off by the paramedics, Barton tossed a carrier bag to a bystander," Ruth said. "What's the betting it contained drugs? The kids I speak to at the centre are pretty sure there is a gang war going on. They don't say a lot, but reading between the lines the older teens are very much on one side or the other."

Calladine nodded. "Back to Barton and yesterday's attack. There were others present and we need to find them. The name of whoever buggered off with that bag would be useful."

"Easier said than done," Ruth said. "People are scared, and Barton in particular has a lot of clout on the estate. Never forget, he is one of them."

"We mustn't lose sight of the alleged gang war on the Hobfield, but another dimension to the Crosby killing has come to light at the post-mortem." Calladine tapped the bundle of files on the desk in front of him. "Most of you won't remember, but twenty-three years ago there was a series of murders on the estate attributed to a killer known only as the 'Shadow'. He had a hallmark, he carved the letter 'X' somewhere on the victim's body. Crosby has one on his back, and that is too much of a coincidence." He looked at Alice. "I want you to go through these files, make a list of the victims' names, their relatives and anyone we interviewed, then we'll speak to them. Don't say anything that links it to the Crosby murder. If anyone asks why the renewed interest, tell them it's research for another case, nothing more."

He addressed two of the uniformed officers. "I want you out and about on the Hobfield. Find out who was present when Barton was stabbed, and log what they saw. You never know, someone might let something slip about the bag he threw to a bystander. Like Ruth says, what's the betting it contained drugs."

"Rocco, Alice, I know you've already done some research but look again, dig deep into the backgrounds of both Spooner and Barton. Currently, Barton is working at Goddard's garden centre. Given that he's a strong contestant in the race for the estate, we should have a word. Ruth and I will pay him a visit shortly. Rocco, get on to communications and find out where they are with Noah's mobile. If you get anything, ring me. Also, look up an incident for me, the one where Killian Seddon was attacked. Speak to the officer who attended. Killian will have gone to hospital, so there should be records."

For a few seconds he watched the team making notes. He'd missed this. All those days spent at home with his feet up — this was what he'd been itching for. He needed a case to get stuck into, get his brain cells in shape, and this one would fill the gap nicely.

The team was busy at their desks making notes and setting about their allocated tasks. Ruth went to the front of the room and joined Calladine. "What about Kitty's office?" Ruth asked. "Are we looking into that?"

"Yes, but quietly and without attracting attention," he said. "A disgruntled customer is bad enough but this could be something else, something more sinister."

"Like what?" Ruth asked.

"Let's see what we find out first. Check where Barton is today, if he's at home or has managed to go back to work. After our visit, you and I will take a walk round to those units at the back of the library and ask if any of the other business owners have suffered any intimidation recently."

"Anything in particular in mind?" she asked.

"Yes, having their premises shot at with a rifle."

* * *

Pulling out of the nick car park, Ruth made a quick call to the garden centre, who confirmed that Barton was back at work. "You're talking about a protection racket." She waited until they were almost at Goddard's before coming out with that little gem.

"It's a possibility. Kitty isn't usually so coy. Her refusal to talk to me about the incident yesterday has got me wondering."

"Yes, but who is likely to be behind something like that?" she asked doubtfully.

"I can think of any number of people. Problem is, I've locked most of them up."

"D'you think it's got anything to do with the trouble on the estate?" Ruth asked.

"Who knows, but it's very different from the knife attacks."

"Apart from the balaclava," she reminded him. "Do we know anything about the Goddards or their workforce?"

"The family is Lena Goddard and her son Marcus," Calladine said. "Mark Goddard, who started the business, is doing a long prison stretch. I was on the team that put him there nine years ago and I'm afraid his wife Lena blames me."

"That's hardly fair. How long did he get?" Ruth asked.

"Twenty-five years. He shot and killed someone during a jewellery store robbery."

"Then the sentence is justified," she said.

"That's not how Lena sees it, I'm afraid," Calladine said. "Him and his gang were arrested. Once they realised how serious the charge was, the other gang members pointed the finger at Goddard. Swore on oath that it'd been him carrying the gun. He was found guilty and sentenced, same as most criminals who are subject to the due process of law."

As they got out of the car, Ruth was in thoughtful mode. "Are you saying that the money for this little lot was paid for with ill-gotten gains?"

"Very likely. I doubt that was the first robbery Mark Goddard was responsible for. A lot of what he amassed was confiscated under proceeds of crime, but no doubt he had plenty more salted away over the years. I reckon this business was originally set up as a cover."

"And today?"

"As far as we're aware, neither Lena nor Marcus have given us any trouble," Calladine said.

"But they do employ Luke Barton, who is allegedly making a play for the Hobfield."

Calladine nodded. "We'll bear it in mind."

A man spoke from behind them. "You're police. And you're the copper who was bothering me yesterday." This was aimed at Ruth.

Calladine spun round, smiled and showed him his badge. "Indeed we are, Mr Barton.

The young man gave him a quick scowl, then turned his attention to Ruth. "I've seen you around a lot lately. As well as being police, you're that woman from the youth club."

Ruth nodded. "If you fancy joining, I'm afraid you're a little old. Unless you're volunteering to help, of course."

"Wouldn't be seen dead in that place," he scoffed.

"Don't you fancy helping out with the youth of the estate? It's where you were brought up, after all," Calladine said.

"Brought up? Dragged up more like."

"Rumour these days has it that you fancy your chances at running it — well, running the dealing that goes on there anyway."

Barton laughed. "Rumours, Mr Calladine. Take no notice of Hobfield chat. You know what that place is like. Anyway I don't mess with drugs, and as for the estate, I can't wait to get out of the place. Working here for the Goddards is no picnic, and it doesn't leave me time for an alternative enterprise even if I fancied it, which I don't. So, what can I do for you?"

"You can tell us about the knife attack yesterday," Ruth said.

"I already told you, I was set upon by some strange bloke dressed in black. I didn't get a good look at him. All I saw was a dark shadow on the ground, I swivelled round and he got me with the blade."

"Description?"

"I've no idea, he had a balaclava on, so I could only see his eyes. But the knife was one of those big kitchen jobs."

"We've had a couple of uniformed officers asking questions on the estate and we know there were witnesses. A few lads admitted they were hanging about when you were attacked, but they don't seem to be able to describe the man," Ruth said.

"They might have been there but I didn't see them. And even if I had, it's more than my life's worth to name names. You know what this place is like. I spill my guts to you lot and the next time I get jumped it'll be twice as bad. Look, I'd met up with some mates and was about to leave them to it. I was making my way towards the alley that leads to the back field when he struck."

"Weren't you working that day?" Calladine asked.

"It was my day off and I was catching up with friends. That's allowed, isn't it, even on the Hobfield?"

Calladine nodded. "Fair enough, but what about others on the estate, those who're not your friends? We know there's currently a battle going on for control of that estate. Who's your rival? Ricky Spooner? We know there's no love lost between the pair of you. Was it one of his mob who jumped you?"

"Look, you might as well stop hassling me 'cause I'm not telling you anything. Me and Spook, we try to keep out of each other's way. It keeps things simple," Barton said.

"Well, you upset someone. If it wasn't Spooner, d'you have any other ideas?" Calladine asked.

"It wasn't Spook. An attack with a knife isn't his style. His morons use baseball bats to beat the crap out of anyone who crosses them."

He sounded so sure it puzzled Calladine. "That sounds like the voice of experience. Have you crossed Spooner before?"

"Not recently. I don't look for trouble and Spook is just that, an idiot with money and a huge chip on his shoulder. He's best left alone. I don't like the guy but I don't court trouble either."

"How is the arm?" Ruth asked.

"It'll heal, but the scar will look a bit weird."

"Why's that then?" asked Calladine. "Didn't the doctor stitch it up right?"

"He did his best but it was a tricky call. The attacker lunged at me from behind but I heard him, sensed something. I put my arm up to shield my body and he nicked my shoulder. I was shocked, I had no idea what was going on. Then next thing he uses the blade to draw an 'X' shape on my forearm."

Calladine said nothing but Barton's words filled him with dread. They had another one. So much for the marks being a coincidence. "You threw something to a bystander, a witness who may be able to help us. Who was that?"

Barton shrugged. "I thought it was a robbery. I was carrying a present for my mother. Nothing special, just a box of chocolates. It was a reaction, that's all."

"Names," Calladine insisted. "There was a group with you, they saw what happened. You might be reluctant but we need their names. Their statements could be crucial."

"Can't remember, sorry, the whole incident is a bit of a blur."

"You didn't know the man who attacked you?" Calladine asked.

"If I did I'd be on his tail. Believe me, if I had a name I'd give it to you."

Barton wasn't being helpful but there wasn't much they could do about it. "He might try again," Ruth warned him. "It's in your own interests to talk to us, Luke."

He smiled at her. "I'll take my chances. I hear anything on the streets or around town, you'll be the first to know."

"Perhaps you can help with something else. We're investigating the murder of Noah Crosby. He worked here part-time, I believe," she said.

The sound of Noah's name wiped the smile off his face. "I didn't see much of him at work. He annoyed the management with his swearing and bad attitude. Folk like that don't last long in this kind of business. The public don't like it."

"Odd that, we were told you got on, that Noah had switched sides," Ruth said. "Ditched Spooner's gang and moved to yours."

Another scowl. "Tittle tattle, Sergeant. We've already dealt with that. I don't have a gang, nor do I have anything to do with Spooner."

"What d'you know about Noah Crosby?" Calladine said.

"Like me, he lived on the estate. I caught sight of him occasionally but as for working here, you'd be better off asking Marcus."

"Marcus Goddard, the owner?"

"The owner's son," Barton said. "Noah worked here a couple of half days a week, and Marcus usually found a use for him. They drank together occasionally, too."

"Drank?" Ruth said. "Noah was only sixteen."

Barton grinned. "Never bothered Noah or Marcus, and if it bothered anyone else they never said owt. Mind you, with Marcus in tow they wouldn't dare."

CHAPTER TWELVE

Luke Barton showed Calladine and Ruth to the office. Marcus Goddard was sitting at a desk, speaking to someone on his mobile. He saw the group approach, yawned and put the phone in his jacket pocket.

"Police," Barton said.

Marcus pointed to Calladine. "You're the plod who put my dad away. My mother never tires of telling me how much she hates you for that." He grinned. "Any mention of you winds her up no end."

"Your father was a villain and deserved everything he got. And I didn't put him away, the court did."

"Fair comment, but my mother still blames you and there's no shaking her."

"We're here about Noah Crosby," Ruth interrupted. "Can you tell us when you last saw him?"

"Poor lad. I heard you found him rotting in an alleyway on the Hobfield." Marcus shuddered. "Truth is, I rarely saw him at all. Four weekends ago I gave him twenty quid to clean my car. Can't say I've seen him since."

"D'you have an exact date?" Calladine asked.

"No, but it was a Saturday, and he didn't do a bad job as it happens." He smiled. "There's not a lot more I can say. He was a shifty looking lad though. I told Luke to keep an eye on him and not to let him near the tills."

"Barton tells me he didn't have much to do with the lad here, that you organised his work. What did you have him doing?" Calladine asked.

"All sorts — unloading and shifting plants. Carrying the heavy stuff to customers' cars, that type of thing."

"You drank with him occasionally," Calladine said.

Marcus laughed. "Very occasionally. The lad was fond of that dive on the Hobfield. We went there a couple of times."

"Didn't you find the Wheatsheaf a bit out of your comfort zone?"

"No, Detective. One or two who drink in there knew my dad. They talk to me, tell me about his escapades. My mother won't talk about that aspect of Dad's life. She believes he's innocent and was wrongly imprisoned, so if I want the truth, I have to go elsewhere."

"You have no illusions about your father then?" Ruth asked.

"No, Sergeant. He's a villain, pure and simple, and now he's paying his debt to society."

Calladine thought Marcus Goddard seemed like a straightforward sort of young man. He answered their questions and wasn't shy about talking about his dad's dubious reputation. "You also employ Luke Barton. How d'you find him?"

"Luke's okay, a good worker and trustworthy. Why? What's he been up to?"

Trustworthy? Surely he must know about his reputation. He knew enough about everything else. Calladine shook his head. "Nothing that I'm aware of, but we have our suspicions."

Marcus smirked. "Anything I should know about?"

"Is there anyone here Noah would have been pally with?" Ruth asked. "Perhaps someone nearer his own age."

"Not really, he wasn't the type to make friends. But he was a good worker and amusing when we went drinking. I know he was known locally as a scally. Living on that damned estate tends to taint people."

Neither Calladine nor Ruth wanted to get into a debate about the problems on the Hobfield.

"Thanks," Ruth said.

Calladine handed him a card. "If you think of anything else that might help, give me a ring."

"Aren't you going to say hello to my mum while you're here? I could do with a laugh and she's in a right old mood today."

Calladine regarded the young man. "Not on this visit, but do tell her I called and that it might be necessary to return."

"You're welcome anytime, Inspector, as an investigator or customer. Your money's as good as anyone's."

"What did you make of him?" Ruth asked on their way back to the car.

"Seems straightforward enough, doesn't take stuff too seriously. Very different from his mother. Life on the wrong side of Lena isn't a comfortable place, far too dangerous. Threatened me with all sorts when the judge sentenced Mark."

"What d'you think, is either Goddard or Barton involved in Noah's murder?" she asked.

"Hard to say, but neither of them struck me as being particularly bothered by us."

"How about Barton and Spooner? What's the story there d'you think?"

"Might just be Hobfield chat like Barton said. How did he strike you?" Calladine said.

Ruth thought for a moment. "I'm not sure, but Noah must have upset someone and we're running out of possibilities."

Calladine looked around while he considered this. The centre took up a large area. There was a shop and a café, plus the outside space with plants and gardening paraphernalia. There were plenty of people milling around too — a good little business.

"We still don't have a motive for the lad's murder. He upset someone, but who? We've still got a lot to learn about that young man," he said.

Ruth nodded. "As far as the Goddard family are concerned, this is a legitimate business. Would Marcus turn a blind eye to one of his employees dealing? He might, but then again he wouldn't want us breathing down his neck and his mother wouldn't want that good reputation they've spent time and money building spoiling either."

She was right. Nonetheless, Calladine would keep the garden centre and the Goddards in mind. "We need to build a timeline of Noah's movements over the last few days of his life."

Ruth nodded. "We're not yet sure of the dates of his last days. Okay, gut reaction, what d'you think happened to him? Did he get caught up in a gang war, or perhaps he was knifed by that blast from the past who likes to carve marks in flesh? According to Killian's mum we should be looking for someone who's been away but is now back on our patch."

"Don't joke about the Shadow, Ruth. I was a DS back then, still learning the job, and it wasn't a good time. My DI took the lack of progress personally. Eventually he had a nervous breakdown and retired."

"Sorry, the last thing I want to do is upset you, but finding that mark on Noah is weird, and then the incident with Barton. It has to be a coincidence surely?"

Calladine could only hope she was right. "Let's go and have a word with Spooner. See what he can throw into the mix. If he and Barton really are rivals, then Spooner has a motive for going after Barton."

Calladine didn't say much on the drive. "What's eating you?" Ruth asked. "The case, or the imminent return of Amy?"

"Both, Ruth. The case is turning into a nightmare and as for Amy, she's bound to cause problems."

"Why? You're with Kitty now. Amy will have to get used to the idea."

Oh if only it was that simple! The fact of the matter was that Calladine was still fond of Amy. She could easily slip back into his life and he wouldn't complain. That left him doubting his true feelings for Kitty.

"You still like her, don't you? That's what's doing your head in. Amy moves back and she's part of your life whether you like it or not. Maisie is related by blood to you both, and you can't avoid each other."

"Am I that transparent?"

"Yes, and if I can see right through you, so will Kitty. You need to sort out your emotions before Amy gets here," Ruth said.

CHAPTER THIRTEEN

Ruth pulled up outside the Spooner house. "Let's hope he's in a cooperative mood," she said.

"It's in his own interests. We know he and Barton are rivals, which makes him a possible suspect."

Ruth rang the doorbell and the two waited. The housekeeper, a middle-aged woman, answered.

"We'd like a quick word with Ricky," Calladine said.

She showed them inside. Ricky Spooner was in the sitting room, slouched on the sofa.

After the introductions, Ruth asked, "Can you tell us where you were yesterday afternoon?"

Spooner glared at them both. "Why? What's it got to do with you?"

"Luke Barton was attacked, and we're reliably told the pair of you don't get on." Calladine gave him a quick smile. "We're asking everyone who might have seen it."

Spooner gave the pair an odd look, then he smirked. "I was at the showroom in Oldston all day. Ask any of the staff, they can all vouch for me."

"You're sure you were nowhere near the Hobfield, not even during your lunch hour?" she said.

"Nope." He grinned. "I took a valued customer to the 'Old Barn' restaurant for lunch, you can ask them too. Sorry, but you're looking for someone else, it definitely wasn't me who knifed that idiot."

"We didn't say he was attacked with a knife," Ruth said. "So who told you?"

He shrugged. "Someone must have said something, or maybe I read about it on social media. You know what these things are like. Some poor sod gets stabbed, particularly on the Hobfield, and it goes viral around Leesdon within the hour."

"When did you see Barton last?" she asked.

"I don't see him. Our paths don't cross as a rule."

"Another rumour has you and Barton locked in conflict over who runs the Hobfield," Calladine said.

"I want nowt to do with the place. As far as I'm concerned, Barton wants it then it's all his. He's welcome to it."

Calladine didn't know whether to believe him or not. He'd reserve judgement until he'd checked the young man's alibis. "Noah Crosby, know him?"

"Young Noah, yes, I'd seen him about."

"When was the last time you saw him?"

"Look, I can't remember, and anyway it would only have been in passing. He wasn't someone I spent time with." He grinned again. "Now, have you done, because I've got to be at the showroom."

Calladine nodded. "Fair enough, but we'll probably want to speak to you again."

* * *

Back in the car, Calladine said, "I'm calling it a day. I should get home, see if Kitty is ready to tell me the truth about who shot at her window."

"If someone is leaning on her, she'll be afraid so tread careful."

"I'm not stupid. But if that is what's happening, I'd hope she'd talk to me about it," he said.

"You don't know what she's been threatened with. Have you considered that it could have something to do with a case she's working on, that she could have stumbled on something?"

"Like what?" Calladine asked.

"Something the shooter doesn't want her talking about."

"I asked her that, if it was a client or someone she was chasing that she'd annoyed and she said not. I'm not a mind reader, Ruth. She talks to me or we've got a job on."

"There's still the protection racket theory," she said.

"We need that one reinforcing or quashing, and quick. We'll have that talk to Billy Knowles's dad first thing tomorrow," Calladine said.

CHAPTER FOURTEEN

Thursday

Thursday was one of Calladine's early morning gym sessions, but his heart wasn't in it. He'd too much to do and think about. The case was tricky and work was piling up.

"You home for tea?" Kitty asked as she collected her things ready to leave. "Only I might be late. I'm seeing a client at six and it could take a while."

"No problem. I'll get something on my way home."

"Not a takeaway," she insisted. "There's cold chicken in the fridge, put some salad with it and that should do you."

He'd turn into a bloody chicken salad if things didn't change.

"I've left those colour charts and samples on the sideboard. I think you should paper all four walls in the sitting room. A good quality paper will cover a multitude of sins."

"There's nowt wrong with my walls," he said.

"There's any number of cracks and bumps. Just get it papered, Tom. Something neutral. I've left the sample book open at the one I like."

"I take it you're still not ready to talk about the window."

"No, Tom, I told you I'd sort it."

"And have you?"

"Not yet, I just need to weigh up a few options."

"Options? I reckon you should add me to that list. Whoever shot at your office needs hauling in and charging," he said.

The front door slammed shut. Kitty still wasn't up for discussing the matter. He was left sitting on the sofa next to Sam. He tickled the dog's neck and let out a weary sigh. "What're we to do with her, eh, boy? Why won't she trust me?"

He was about to leave for the station when his mobile rang. It was Ruth. She was already at her desk.

"Billy Knowles has been in tears again. Jake had to send him home yesterday afternoon. The lad was tight lipped, wouldn't explain why he was so upset, but he told his best mate that he wouldn't be living in Leesdon for much longer."

"We'll visit those units first thing. I'll walk round, the exercise will do me good. I'll meet you outside the library shortly. We need that word with his dad. If someone is leaning on him, we need to find out who."

"And Kitty, is she a victim of this harassment too?"

"Can't get a word out of her either. Reckons she'll sort it herself."

"Nothing you can do then."

"Oh yes there is," he retorted. "Someone fired a rifle in the High Street in the middle of the day. I can't let that go. I want forensics to take a look at Kitty's office and I want uniform up and down that street asking questions. They can do the shops, we'll look at offices and works. Get it organised before you leave the nick. Anyone shows the slightest sign of being the victim of a protection racket we push for answers, got that?"

"You're in a right mood this morning. Not had your breakfast?"

"I'm fine. I think it's the stress of the case. I missed work but I'd forgotten how hard it is."

* * *

He was right, the ten minute walk cleared his head. Calladine stood in the library car park waiting for Ruth, feeling decidedly guilty about the way he'd spoken to her.

"Uniform are on the job as we speak, forensics too. You have told Kitty they're coming?"

He shook his head. No he hadn't, but he didn't care. As far as he was concerned, it was out of her hands. "Sorry for being so ratty. I'm letting the job get to me and I shouldn't."

"Don't worry about me. Jibes from you are water off a duck's back, but something's wrong. I'm presuming Kitty's not playing the game. If she won't talk to you, it could mean that someone's piling on the pressure."

"I agree, and it's doing my head in. Let's go and speak to Rob Knowles, see if he's going to hold out on us too," Calladine said.

The door to Knowles's unit was locked up tight, the blinds drawn, but there was a light on inside. Calladine rapped on the door and called out, "Police, Mr Knowles, can you open the door?"

"What d'you want?" a voice shouted back.

"A word, and it's important."

Several minutes later, Knowles peered out through the blinds at the window. Calladine held up his warrant card, hoping it would reassure the man. Finally, he opened the door to them.

"Why so guarded, Mr Knowles? Anyone would think you were scared of something — or perhaps it's someone."

The words had him flustered. His face reddened and he shook his head. "I'm just busy, that's all. I've got stock to sort out. I'm doing Oldston market tomorrow."

Ruth smiled. "We won't keep you long. We're speaking to as many businesses in the town as we can."

"Why? What's going on?" Knowles said.

"We believe a number of businesses are being harassed, even threatened, if money isn't paid over," she said.

He backed off, his eyes wide. "I don't know what you're talking about. I'm perfectly fine."

"Mr Knowles, if you're being leaned on, for money or anything else, we can help, protect you from whoever is doing this," Calladine said.

"I told you, I'm fine, just stressed sorting this lot out."

Calladine cast his eyes around the unit. There was a great deal of shelving and a table against one wall packed high with trainers in boxes. "I'm after a new pair of those for the gym. The ones I've got are knackered."

"Size?" Knowles asked.

Calladine squinted at one of the boxes. "Those look about right."

Knowles opened the window and thrust the box at him. "Now go I'm seen talking to you lot, they'll torch the place."

Calladine groaned inwardly. Knowles's words had confirmed what he'd suspected. This had to be a protection racket. Not only did they have a madman with a knife on the loose, but they now had someone demanding money with menaces. Tired of calling through the window, he pushed his way in. "I seriously advise you to talk to us. You are not alone, I'm aware of another business in the same position as you. I can have your premises watched."

"Sorry, I can't talk to you. I've got this place to think about and a family to feed."

Calladine opened the box and examined the trainers. They were expensive looking. He couldn't be sure but they looked like the pair found on Noah's body. "How much?"

"Have them on the house. Now, please go."

Calladine smiled. "I want to pay for them. Forty do it?"

Knowles snatched the money from his hand and nodded at the door. "If you don't mind, I've got work to do."

Calladine tucked the box under his arm and made for the door.

"We should let Julian have a look at those," Ruth said, once they were outside.

"I had just the same thought."

"The trainers Noah was found in were in a right state but they look the same to me," she said.

He nodded. "They could be, we'll have to check."

"This could be important, Tom. What you've got there costs anything from six to eight hundred pounds depending on where you shop. They're top of the range and Knowles had at least two dozen pairs in there."

"What're you getting at?" he asked.

"Stock like that costs money and it's not usually sold on a market stall."

"They'll be lookalikes, not the real thing," he said.

Ruth took the box from him and examined one of the trainers. "They've got the designer label on them, they look the business to me. Something isn't right, Tom. The top sports shops don't stock many pairs of these, can't afford to, and Knowles had loads of them."

"What're you saying?"

Ruth put the shoe back in the box and gave it to him. "I don't know, perhaps they are fake. I'm no expert. But fake or not, we need to know where Knowles got them."

Calladine remained silent, he was playing with another theory. Finally, he said, "Or they're stolen, and somehow Knowles got hold of some. Perhaps that's why he's being leaned on."

"Possibly, or perhaps they're just seconds," Ruth suggested. "What d'you think? Is he a victim of a protection racket or not?"

"You heard him, Ruth. He thinks the place will get torched if he speaks to us. There is something going on, but I'm not sure what. Someone needs to speak to us or we won't get off first base. I'll have uniform keep an eye on these units, particularly after dark," Calladine said.

"Where to now?" Ruth asked.

"We'll give Knowles time to think about it. Meanwhile, another word with Kitty, and this time I won't be swayed by her dismissive attitude."

CHAPTER FIFTEEN

Kitty was in no mood to talk protection racket or anything else. She was busy, working on her laptop with the office phone tucked under her chin.

"I'll be with you within the hour," she said, replacing the receiver. Turning to the pair, she gave them a half-hearted smile. "I've no time for idle chit chat, Tom. Too much to do."

"Me too, love, but we have to discuss your window. I can't just let it drop."

"It's all mended now, so what's the point?"

"You're not the only business in this town being targeted. We've just come from talking to someone who's every bit as terrified as you are."

She stared back at him with angry eyes. "I'm not terrified, Tom. Just fed up to the back teeth of the way you keep going on and on. It was an accident, what more can I say?"

"It was no accident, and I need to find whoever was behind it."

"It was school kids, go and bother them," she said.

"No, someone shot at the window, therefore it was deliberate. Courtesy of Mary across the road, I have the shooter on film. He parked up and deliberately targeted your premises. Want to talk to me now?"

She glared at him. "No, you've got it all wrong."

Calladine heaved a sigh, gestured to Ruth and made for the door. "Forensics are on their way. They'll give the place a thorough going over and then we'll talk again."

"What do they hope to find?" Kitty asked.

"The bullet will do for starters." He looked at the trajectory from the upper window to the back wall. "I reckon it's buried up there where the plaster has come away."

"So what? It's a bullet, what can that tell you?"

"You'd be surprised."

He beckoned again to Ruth and the pair left.

"Not much we can do if she won't talk to us," Ruth said. "Exactly like Knowles. I'd like to know what is going on though. Protection is just one possibility, but how much money do the crooks hope to get from them? I doubt either of the businesses is making a fortune."

"Kitty just about breaks even," Calladine said.

"We'll keep an open mind."

They were making for Ruth's car in the library car park when someone called out.

"Tom!"

Calladine would have known Amy's soft tone anywhere. He turned to Ruth and smiled. "You get back to the station, I'll catch up with you later."

"Don't let Kitty see you," she warned, walking off. "She thinks you're seeing Amy again she'll skin you alive. You've got five minutes. I'll wait for you in the car."

Amy Dean crossed the road, put her arms around Calladine and gave him a big hug. "You look well, you're in good shape, very different from last time I saw you."

Amy looked lovely, bright-eyed and with her lustrous hair caught in a loose ponytail. She still wore the vivid colours and long skirts he remembered from their time together. He clapped his belly. "Exercise, and the diet, seems to be paying dividends."

"I've been out for a walk with Zoe and the baby. Gosh she's grown, and she gave me a smile."

Calladine nodded in approval but he felt miffed. Lately he'd got the impression that Zoe was excluding him from his granddaughter's life, and he didn't like it.

"Julian said you were visiting."

"Moving back, Tom," she corrected. "And I can't wait. Having a new addition in the family, little Maisie to dote on, how could I not?"

"Have you got a place?"

"I'll stay with Julian in his apartment for the time being. He's hardly ever home anyway." She laughed. "That young man is always working. Leave that lab of his for too long and he gets withdrawal symptoms."

"What about your business? Will you start up again?"

"Questions, questions. You're back in the old routine, I see."

She was right, he was asking too much and too soon. "I'm curious, that's all. There's not a lot of premises available in the villages."

"Not important, my trade is online mostly these days, and I like it that way. It means I'm not tied to a shop eight hours a day like before. Look, we've got tons of catching up to do, how about having dinner with me one night this week? We can go to that lovely new bistro by the river."

Kitty's reaction played out in his mind and made him squirm. There was no way she'd be happy with him seeing an ex, particularly this one, and she had a hellava temper when the occasion arose. "You do know I'm with someone." The words were out before he could bite them back. Worse than that, he wished they weren't true. What had got into him? Amy was an old flame, she belonged in his past, so why the nerves and the regret?

"Yes, Julian told me." She looked into his eyes and smiled. "I'm told this Kitty is very nice, but she's not for you." She said this with a shake of the head and a degree of certainty that made him shiver. "You forget, Tom, I'm a seer, I know things. Your future life partner is someone you already know, but it's not her."

Did she mean herself? He couldn't tell from the look on Amy's face. To mask his confusion, he said, "I'd better go, work to do, you know how it is."

"I know how it is with you, Tom. Think about that dinner. I'll ring you in the week."

CHAPTER SIXTEEN

"You've got that dreamy look on your face again."

"Keep out of my private life and drive, Bayliss. You know nothing."

"I know you're still into Amy, you can't help yourself. Kitty's not daft, you know, she'll spot the change in you and want all the gory details."

Ruth was right. With Amy back on the scene permanently, Kitty was bound to have her doubts. She knew how fond he'd been of Amy.

"Why is Kitty lying to us?" Ruth asked. "As you pointed out, she can hardly make a fortune from that PI business of hers, just makes ends meet if she's lucky. So, what does whoever's leaning on her hope to gain?"

Good question. Calladine didn't have an answer. "Knowles is in the same boat. He's a market trader, works hand to mouth. If both of them refuse to say anything, we're left relying on more victims coming forward."

"It's hard to believe that Amy and Julian are closely related," Ruth said, changing the subject. "They're so very different — Julian's all science and logic and Amy never leaves home without a pack of Tarot cards in her bag."

"Look, d'you mind if we leave Amy out of our conversations until I've decided which way things are going?"

"I knew it! You still like her. I almost feel sorry for Kitty now," Ruth cried.

"We've got better things to concentrate on than my love life. Noah's killer — forgotten that one?"

The conversation was edging towards the tricky when Calladine's mobile rang. It was Alice Bolshaw back at the station.

"We've had a man ring in, sir. One Ahmed Khan, he owns the late night shop on the Oldston Road. He's seen the article in the paper about Noah Crosby and reckons he has some information."

"Text me his address and Ruth and I will get round there. Have uniform returned with any information for us?"

"PC Tomlinson reckons that the owner of the sportswear shop on the precinct was cagey. He's worth another visit."

Calladine noted it down. "Thanks, Alice. Looks like we'll be out of the station for a while."

* * *

Ahmed Khan apologised for not getting in touch with the police before now. "I had no idea the young man was dead. I saw the report in the local paper and rang you straight away."

"You told a colleague that the person who robbed you wore a horror mask," Ruth said. "Can you recall what it looked like?"

"He did, it had a zombie-type face, all teeth, peeling skin and blood, but from the way he walked, I could tell he was young. I tried to stop him. At one point he lunged at me and I tried to pull the mask away. He didn't expect it. He hit my side with a bat and I backed off. He filled a bag with the cigarettes off my shelves and made a dash for the door. I grabbed the first thing to hand," he gave a shrug, "not that it helped, a bag of flour would you believe? A can or bottle would have been more effective."

"When you reported the theft, did you mention the flour?"

"Yes, I told the young constable. He thought it was amusing but he obviously has no idea how frightening an experience like that can be."

"Can you recall when this was?" Ruth asked.

"Yes, exactly three weeks and two days ago. I remember because I dropped my sister off at the airport the following morning. Look, I didn't hurt him, I never got close enough. I read that he'd been found dead and panicked that it might have something to do with the robbery."

"His death has nothing to do with you, Mr Khan," Ruth said. "Did he have anyone with him?"

"I gave chase and saw him jump into a van parked at the end of the street. All I know is that it was a man driving and they left at speed."

"Make? Colour?" Calladine asked.

"A navy transit type," Mr Khan said.

"Thanks, that's very helpful." Ruth smiled at him.

Calladine thought so too but he didn't know what to make of it. Was Noah behind all the late shop robberies? And the man who'd helped Noah, the one who drove the getaway vehicle, a blue transit type van. Was that the same man who'd shot at Kitty's office window?

CHAPTER SEVENTEEN

That afternoon, Calladine gathered the team together for an update. First, he turned to Alice Bolshaw. "Have you found anything new or interesting about either Spooner or Barton?"

Alice adjusted her glasses and referred to her notes. "Ricky Spooner, good home and schooling, overbearing mother." She smirked. "He's had the odd caution and was done for speeding last year. He does hang out on the Hobfield. One night two months ago he was stopped by a uniformed officer and asked what he was carrying in a sports bag. There had been a drugs bust in one of the flats and uniform was targeting anyone they spotted. But he was clean. The sports bag only contained several pairs of trainers."

Calladine noted it on the incident board. "Trainers again. The market trader, Knowles, had loads of pairs in his lock-up. I'm not sure what it means but we'll find out."

"Branded, were they?" asked Rocco.

Ruth tossed him the pair Calladine had been given. "Yes, and expensive in the sports shops."

They watched while Rocco examined them closely. "These look genuine enough but they have to be fakes, or what're they doing on a market stall?"

"They'll be seconds, surely?" Calladine said.

"Hard to say. I can't see anything obviously wrong with them."

Calladine had a problem. Should he tackle Knowles, ask him outright where he got them or pass the matter to Trading Standards? "We'll pay Knowles another visit," he told Ruth. "Find out where he got them from and what price he's selling them for. If these are seconds, he should make that plain to his customers. We've enough to do right now without getting too involved but we'll tell uniform to keep an eye on him."

Calladine pointed to the board, and the important stuff. "Prior to being murdered, Noah was robbing the late night shop on the Oldston Road. It was the owner who threw the flour at him. We have an exact date for the robbery, and given Noah wasn't seen after that and that his clothing was covered in flour, probably the night he was killed. I'm thinking that after the robbery he was dropped off on the Hobfield, his mate drove off and Noah met his killer." He looked at Alice. "Anything on Noah's mobile yet?"

Alice waved a sheet of paper. "Every call and text to and from that mobile over the last three months."

Calladine nodded. He'd take a look shortly. "His social media?"

"Very little activity, sir. The odd tweet about football, that's it."

Calladine was about to ask her something else when DS Don Thorpe interrupted. He stood slouched against the office door and beckoned to the DI. "We've had a call, sir," he began. "Anonymous, some scroat off the Hobfield, lay odds on it. He says he saw the Crosby lad being dropped off and glimpsed his attacker."

"Name?"

Thorpe shook his head. "No such luck, but he did say the van was a navy blue transit."

The same van Mary had described the shooter as driving. Were these cases linked? Calladine had that familiar sinking feeling in his stomach.

"And he took a photo with his mobile." Thorpe tapped a few keys on his phone and Calladine's pinged in his pocket. "I've texted it to you. Not very good, I'm afraid. The informant reckons he was too scared to use the flash. And before you ask, we've tried to trace the number, but no luck. It's an unregistered pay as you go."

Wasn't that always the way? Calladine had a look. Thorpe was right, the image wasn't the best. "Alice, I'll send this to you. Get it cleaned up, printed out and pin it on the board next to another one I'll give you." He wanted to compare the two vehicles, see if there was any possibility of getting even a partial of the licence number.

"Did your informant give you anything else?"

Thorpe shook his head. "If I do get anything, I'll be sure to pass it on."

Calladine nodded to one of the uniforms to close the door after him. "Rocco, tomorrow morning take two PCs and have a look at those empty flats on the ground floor of Heron House. It's possible Noah was dossing down in one of them. Alice, carry on looking at the Shadow files. Any familiar names crop up, let me know at once."

He held out his hand for the sheet listing the mobile calls. Alice had ringed some and labelled them.

"The phone was on contract, not a burner. All his contacts are listed. During the last week of his life, Noah rang his mother, the Indian takeaway on Leesdon High street and one other number listed in his contacts as Luke Barton. I've checked the number and it's a pay as you go, not registered to anyone."

"How many calls did Noah make to this number?" Calladine asked.

"Dozens, and some of them lasted a while."

Barton had told them that he and Noah didn't get on, that he couldn't take to the lad, so if this was Barton's number, what was going on? "We need another word with him. I suspect Mr Barton wasn't exactly honest about his relationship with Noah."

Ruth smiled. "Bet he'll be pleased to learn that Noah had him listed on his phone. That is if it is Barton's number."

"Comms say the phone is dead," Alice said. "Barton has probably got rid of it by now."

It made sense. With Noah dead, no need for that mobile now. "Someone drove Noah to the late night shop. Given what we've learned from his mobile, that could well be Barton," Calladine said. "We need to pin down that transit van."

This was proving to be a tricky case. No one would talk to them, everyone they interviewed said they had no idea why Noah had been killed. They needed a break, find that vital piece of the jigsaw that would show them the way.

"Right, folks, enough for today," he told the team. "Ruth, first thing tomorrow, you and I will go and lean on Barton. I want to know about his relationship with Noah."

"Rumour has it that Noah had joined Barton's mob, that he'd switched from Spooner to him."

But would that be enough to get him killed? Calladine guessed it all probably depended on what Noah knew about Spooner.

CHAPTER EIGHTEEN

Friday

If there was one place on earth that Rocco detested with all his being, it was the Hobfield estate. He stood in front of Heron House, glanced upwards and shuddered. A while back he'd been clobbered on the head by a young thug who lived in one of the flats and had ended up in hospital with a clot on the brain. He was lucky to be alive. No wonder he experienced such trepidation whenever he visited the estate.

A couple of the flats on the ground floor were legitimately occupied. A single mother with two young kids had one and an elderly couple the other. Neither set of occupants appreciated being disturbed at seven in the morning.

"My lads haven't slept a wink all night," the young mother levelled at them. "Bloody music and cars roaring round at all hours and now you lot making all sorts of noise at the crack of dawn."

"We're not here to disturb you," Rocco said. "We're only interested in the empty flats."

"Well they're not empty, and that's another thing. Bloody homeless and druggies in there every night of the week. Last night someone made a hellava row. There were screaming and shouting until gone two in the morning."

"Can you show me exactly which flat?" Rocco asked.

"The one at the end."

Rocco gestured to the uniforms and made for it. No need to batter the door down this time, it was slightly ajar. Inside they stepped onto a floor covered in empty fast food cartons and beer cans. There were a number of sleeping bags strewn about, on one of them lay a horror mask. Could it be the one Noah Crosby had worn during the robbery? Forensics would soon find out.

"Bag this," he called to one of the uniforms.

"Smells a bit ripe in here, sir."

He was right. The hairs on the back of Rocco's neck began to prickle.

"Seems to be coming from the next room, there." The uniform pointed.

It could be anything, hopefully nothing more than rotting food. Rocco walked forward gingerly into what had once been a bedroom, expecting to see much of the same mess as the room they'd just left. There wasn't much daylight, the curtains were closed tight and the ceiling light didn't work. With every instinct screaming out that something was wrong, he inched forward into the gloom.

A split second later he saw it, a scene right out of a horror film. All Rocco wanted to do in that moment was throw up. Stripped down to his underwear and taped to a chair, he'd been beaten black and blue before being shot in the head. Despite the blood and the bruises, Rocco recognised him from the photographs on the incident board. Rob Knowles.

* * *

Within the hour Natasha Barrington, the pathologist, along with Julian and his team, were on site. Having already examined the scene, Tom Calladine kept to the periphery of the room while they did their work. He'd seen a great deal of brutality during his time at Leesdon nick, and what had been done to Knowles was definitely up there in the top ten. He'd been beaten so badly that all four of the walls in the room were splattered with his blood.

"Until I get him on the slab, it's difficult to say what injuries he sustained, but I can tell you what finished him off," a grim-faced Natasha said. "A bullet to the back of the head."

"But first he was systematically beaten, and suffered numerous blows to the face and head," Calladine added.

"Yes, the knee joints are broken and bloody and they have several puncture holes." She looked at Calladine. "I'm guessing a power drill, poor man."

Ruth Bayliss heard the comment and winced. "This is totally different from what happened to Noah, or the attack on Barton," she whispered. "What the hell is going on?"

"Whoever did this wanted information," Calladine said. "They tortured him mercilessly until they got it."

"We don't know that they did," she said.

"He didn't strike me as a martyr, Ruth."

"I doubt he was. Knowles was a simple working man who ran his own business as well as he could. A market trader with no record and no hint of involvement with drugs, so what made him a target?"

"We'll take another look at that lock-up of his, see if we can find any sort of answer there." Calladine sighed wearily. They'd have to tell the family. He knew from what Ruth had told him that Rob Knowles had a young son. They'd be devastated.

"We'll speak to his wife, get the keys to his lock-up and give it the once over."

"It'd help if we knew what we were looking for," she said.

"I doubt it's drugs, but we'll keep an open mind."

"A young woman, a neighbour, told us she heard a lot of noise last night," one of the uniforms said. "Want me to have a word?"

Calladine shook his head. "No, I'll do it." He gestured to Ruth, and the pair left the scene.

No need to ask which flat the young woman lived in, she was there at the front door, watching events, an infant in her arms.

"Dead, is he?"

Calladine nodded. "Did you get a look at who came to that flat last night?"

"No, and I'd be a fool to tell you lot if I had." She clutched the child tighter and glared at the pair. "I want to live, thanks, which means I daren't have owt to do with you."

"A man was brutally murdered only metres from your front door. Doesn't that bother you?"

"Course it does but I don't want to get involved. Next thing that happens is I'm a target."

With that she went inside and slammed the door shut.

CHAPTER NINETEEN

Brenda Knowles, Rob's wife, worked at Buckley's Pharmaceuticals, one of whose owners was Eve Buckley, Tom Calladine's birth mother. This was a fact he hadn't been privy to until Freda Calladine, the woman he'd believed was his mother, died. Calladine tried to make the best of the situation, but he never felt comfortable in the company of Eve or her family.

On this occasion, though, she proved invaluable. Eve arranged for Brenda Knowles to be taken home and a friend and workmate to remain with her.

"You should try harder with Eve, you know," Ruth said.

"It's not that simple. I think of my mother and the image in my head is Freda. She's the mother who brought me up, not Eve. And don't forget, Eve gave me away. Couldn't cope, so she merrily gave me to someone she didn't even know."

"Come on, let's get it right," Ruth said. "Eve was a teen-age girl who had an affair with your father and got pregnant. It wasn't her fault. And the so-called stranger was Freda, who was married to your father, so she was hardly a stranger. You should be grateful that Freda was the sort of woman who didn't judge too harshly."

"Okay, let's drop it and just agree that the entire thing makes me uncomfortable."

"Regardless of what you feel, Eve's your mother and you should visit her more." She gave him a look. "It's as clear as day that she wants you in her life."

"All right, I am in her life, whether I like it or not. Can we drop it now?"

"I won't say another word." Ruth pulled into the library car park.

"Why would someone torture and murder a man for a few pairs of sports shoes? It makes no sense."

"Nor to me." Ruth was about to unlock the unit doors when she realised that the padlock had been smashed. "Someone beat us to it."

Calladine pushed in front of her, switched on the light and went inside. The place had been turned upside down. There were boxes of goods all over the floor. Shirts, socks and other items of clothing, but no sign of the trainers. "Apologies, Ruth, it looks as if you could be right. Someone came here looking for something and the trainers have gone. There were dozens of boxes of them stacked over there yesterday."

"Why kill over trainers with a dubious pedigree, if that's what they were? I don't understand."

Calladine was rummaging through some boxes at the far end of the unit that had fallen down behind the metal shelving. He opened one and tossed a handbag to Ruth. "What d'you think?"

Ruth's eyes lit up. "Wow! I've seen these advertised on the telly, they're not even on sale yet. These must be literally hot from the factory. Designer bags like this will retail at about a grand when they finally hit the shops." She spent the next few minutes examining the bag closely. "I'm no expert, never having owned one, but it looks the genuine article to me."

"There's another dozen back here. I'm guessing that whoever took the trainers missed these."

"Knowles must have been selling this gear, but is that enough to get him killed?"

"Possibly," Calladine said. "It could be stolen property. If it is, it would depend on who it was stolen from, and given what's happened to him, I doubt that was the original owners."

"You're talking a third party. This stuff gets stolen, stored somewhere and stolen again, and poor Rob Knowles ends up with some choice gear and gets killed for it."

"We don't know the whole story, Ruth, or who is behind this, but as far as I'm aware there've been no local robberies recently involving trainers or designer bags. We keep an open mind."

"The gear could have been stolen elsewhere and is simply being got rid of up here. But there's nothing being said on the streets, we'd have heard. So how do we find out more?"

She had a point.

"We see what other forces have on their books. And don't forget, Noah Crosby had a pair on his feet when he was killed, which gives us a rough timescale."

Ruth looked doubtful. "You think that's the reason he was targeted?"

"We've not found a better one."

"I suggest we have another word with his mates, starting with Dean Seddon. You know what young men are like with trainers and the like. Noah gets his hands on a cheap pair, you can bet your life Dean would have wanted in."

"Good call, let's go and find him." Calladine looked around at the mess. "But first I'd better get forensics down here, give the place the once over."

"Ken Lovell, he's next door. He might know something, seen strangers hanging around."

"He's not there, Ruth. He's round at mine measuring up for the wallpaper. Anyway, he uses that unit of his purely for storage. He doesn't spend his working day in there."

* * *

Dean Seddon was no more welcoming than the last time Calladine and Ruth were at his door. He scowled at the pair and only reluctantly let them in after a warning from his mother.

"Trainers, Dean," Calladine began. "Noah was wearing a fancy pair, expensive too, any idea where he got them from?"

He stared at the floor and then looked at his mum. "Do I have to speak to these?"

"If you know anything just tell them. The sooner they find what they're looking for, the sooner they're gone."

"He got 'em off a mate. I don't know which one, he wouldn't say."

"How long ago?" Ruth asked. "Can you remember?"

"Papers reckon he'd been lying in that alley about three weeks, so not long before that."

"D'you know if any of the other young men on the estate are wearing similar shoes?"

Dean looked at Ruth for a few seconds then shook his head. "That other woman asked me the same question," he said finally.

"What other woman?"

"Nosey bitch, always asking questions. She spoke to Noah about the trainers, then after he disappeared she asked several others."

"Does she have a name?" Calladine asked.

"He's talking about that private investigator from the High Street," Dean's mother butted in. "She was on th'estate all day a few weeks back, asking all the young 'uns about trainers."

Kitty. Had to be, Calladine realised. But why? And was that what got her window shot at? "Why haven't you or your mates got a pair?" he asked.

"Noah reckoned he couldn't get any more. Said he got his as part of a special deal."

"What deal?"

Dean hung his head. "He didn't say, well, not to me anyway. He might have told Barton. He was his best mate back then."

CHAPTER TWENTY

"Whether she likes it or not, Kitty will have to speak to me now."

"You'll end up arguing and get nowhere," Ruth said. "Perhaps you should leave Kitty to me. And you are personally involved, don't forget. Kitty is living with you."

It made sense. Ruth was right. "Okay, I'll wait for you back at the nick, but I want to know everything she tells you, understand?"

Ruth nodded. "Don't worry, I'm not after gory details about your love life, just the shooting and why it happened."

Calladine left Ruth to collect the car and went back to the station on foot. Seeing Rob Knowles like that had shaken him. He'd had time off and it had softened the reality of the brutal nature of the villains they had to deal with. If he was to stay on in the job, he'd have to toughen up.

"Tom!" Amy was waving to him from the other side of the street. She had Maisie in her pram and beckoned him over. "She's just smiled at me. I swear it was the sweetest thing. Isn't she just gorgeous?"

Calladine peered into the pram. The infant was filling out, she had plump, pink cheeks and a dusting of blonde curls covered her head.

"She's going to be a beauty, don't you think?"

He beamed at Amy. "I've missed you." The words were out before he could censor them. *What the hell was he doing? Kitty would kill him if she knew.*

Amy leaned forward and kissed him lightly on the mouth. "And I you."

Calladine momentarily froze and then shook himself. "Sorry, I don't know what came over me. We've had our time, we've both moved on. Trying to regain old ground would be a mistake."

"Why?" she asked softly. "Personally, I'd welcome it. We're family now, I'm not going anywhere and as for moving on, I doubt either of us can do that. We have feelings for each other that neither of us can ditch."

"Kitty," he said. "I have to consider her. She thinks we have a future together."

"And do you?" Amy said. "Or are you playing games as usual?" She shook her head. "I know you of old, Tom Calladine. You do not give your emotions the time they deserve. Think carefully about your future and who you want in it before you do anything rash."

Maisie stirred in her pram and gave a little whimper. "Feeding time," Amy said. "I'd better get her home."

Calladine had a last look at the writhing bundle, stuck his hands in his coat pockets and strode off. He could do without Amy stirring up trouble in his personal life. He was more than capable of doing that himself.

* * *

Kitty Lake took one look at Ruth and went back to studying her computer screen. "I presume he hasn't got the balls to face me himself. He knows I don't want him interfering in my cases, yet he's been dancing round a load of unasked questions for days, and now he sends you."

Ignoring the jibe, Ruth sat down opposite Kitty. "We need your help, or I promise you, this case will drive Tom insane." She was banking on the fact that an appeal to her fondness for him would encourage Kitty to tell her what she knew. "We've got a complicated case on our hands and resources are spread thin, which is why I'm here alone. Apart from which, given your relationship with Tom, it's better that I speak to you rather than him."

"I've already told him," Kitty said wearily. "I don't know who shot at my window."

"Are you sure?" Ruth pressed. "Does your case have anything to do with a man called Rob Knowles, a market trader with a unit behind the library?"

That got Kitty's attention. "It might do."

"Did you speak to him? Perhaps about the stock he was selling, particularly the trainers and designer handbags."

"Why? Is that important?"

"We think it could be. If you have any information, Kitty, you have to tell us."

"I spoke to him briefly over the phone about the matter. Mr Knowles is in my diary for a proper chat later today," she said.

"I'm afraid that won't happen now." Ruth watched the look of annoyance grow on Kitty's face.

"Tom had better not interfere," Kitty said firmly. "He tries to stop me speaking to Knowles and I'll make a complaint."

Ruth thought that rich, given she was Tom's girlfriend. "Knowles was found this morning in an empty flat on the Hobfield, brutally murdered."

Kitty turned pale, she was obviously genuinely shocked. "But why? I spoke to him on the phone earlier in the week. He gave no hint of being in any danger. What did he do, cross the wrong person?"

"We're not sure but we think it has something to do with trainers, which is where you come in."

Kitty picked up a file from her desk and tossed it to Ruth. "Okay, I admit he was part of my investigation. I was told he had a stock of trainers and other designer stuff. All I wanted to know was where he'd got them from. I was hired by Robin Riley, he's the manager of the 'Northern Sportswear' store on the retail park."

Ruth nodded. "I know the place."

"What you might not know is that the shop is just one of a chain of five across the north of England. The other four are situated in retail parks in Manchester, Huddersfield, Lancaster and Leeds. Between them they place orders for tens of thousands of items of sportswear, and their trainer requirement is off the scale."

"Tom and I spoke to Knowles at his unit yesterday. He had a number of boxes in his lock-up which we took to be trainers. D'you have any idea where he got them from?"

"No. That's what Riley hired me to find out. Those trainers are a new line and are not on general release in the shops yet."

That little nugget surprised Ruth. If Kitty was right, then where had the stock in Knowles's lock-up come from? There was only one answer, it had to have been stolen, and high on the list of suspects was Luke Barton. He had worked, albeit briefly, for Northern. But she couldn't share this until they had some proof.

"The manufacturers are selling stock to hand-picked outlets only for the time being, and the local Northern Sportswear shops are five of them. There is a big promotion planned — TV, press, the lot. The new design will go on sale in the selected shops across the country on the same date. It's a really big deal, so you can imagine how upset Riley was when he spotted several youngsters around here already wearing them. Naturally he wants to know where they came from."

"Has he no idea himself?"

"Not a clue and he doesn't want it becoming general knowledge either. He's hoping to sort the problem before it reaches the ears of the area manager, one James Halpin."

"I presume this stock is being held somewhere, ready for distribution."

"Yes, it's safely tucked away in the warehouse awaiting the big day."

"How does Riley know that the trainers he's seen people wearing are the same as the ones he plans to sell?" Ruth asked.

"He's seen samples from the manufacturers, the advertising material, posters and the like. Believe me, he's sure."

"Given what's happened, I'm afraid it's out of his hands now," Ruth said.

"Shame, he was hoping I could find out what happened, retrieve the remaining pairs before too much damage was done."

"Poor Riley, someone around here has beaten Northern Sportswear to it, and got this new range of trainers to the market first. I'm not surprised he's angry," Ruth said.

"It would appear that way, and that is the main thrust of the investigation currently. Riley insists their warehouse hasn't been broken into but that doesn't make sense. For the stuff to be out there, stock must have been stolen." She threw her arms in the air. "I've spoken to Riley, told him my theory but he's insisting that hasn't happened, that all the stock delivered is still present and correct."

Ruth smiled. "Can't be, can it? Not if the local kids are wearing them. A batch must have been stolen, whether Riley will admit it or not. D'you trust him? What's the man like?"

"Believe me, Ruth, he's distraught about what's happened. He's afraid that if Halpin finds out he'll lose his job."

"What I don't understand is why would someone kill over trainers? I just don't get it."

"They're exclusive and expensive," Kitty said. "I have no idea how much stock is missing but it could be worth a small fortune to whoever's got it."

That was a good enough reason to kill. They suspected Barton, but was Knowles involved in the original theft? Ruth didn't think he was the type. Receiving was about his limit. "We'll investigate the possibility of a warehouse robbery," she told Kitty. "All I need is the address."

"The stock earmarked for the local store is kept in a secure room at the rear of the building. No doubt you'll speak to Riley. I'd be interested in knowing what he says to you, and how he explains what's happened to the police."

"Realistically we both know that stock must have been stolen. Riley has to come to terms with that, not least because eventually Northern Sportswear will want to claim on their insurance."

Kitty shrugged. "Perhaps. Did you manage to speak to anyone who bought a pair? I wouldn't mind getting my hands on a sample, see what all the fuss is about."

"That's easy enough, Rob Knowles gave a pair to Tom," Ruth said.

"Tell him to put them somewhere safe and leave them in the box," Kitty said.

"Have you seen any kids wearing them?" Ruth asked.

"Yes, a teenage lad called Killian Seddon was sporting a pair. I offered to buy them but he wasn't for selling. Cost me twenty quid for a few words of information." Kitty frowned. "He said a friend of his, Noah Crosby, had sold them to him. Noah told Seddon to put the word out that he could get his hands on as many pairs as they could sell, and cheap too."

They'd not long since spoken to Killian's brother, Dean, and he'd said nothing about this. That made Ruth angry. She hated being given the run-around, and particularly by teenage kids. "Tom and I saw the boxes in Rob Knowles's lock-up," she told Kitty. "They're all gone now. His place was done over, but whoever took them did leave some designer handbags behind. It strikes me that trainers were not the only items going cheap."

CHAPTER TWENTY-ONE

Calladine was holding one of the trainers Knowles had given him. He turned it over in his hands. "They're either stolen or they're not the genuine article. That's the only logical explanation."

He and Ruth were sitting in his office while Ruth updated him on her conversation with Kitty. "What d'you want to do about Dean? He must know Killian has a pair and he said nothing."

"We'll get to him later. For now we're more interested in his brother." Calladine was still examining the trainers. "Where are these things manufactured?"

"The Far East somewhere, and shipped all over the world."

Calladine took a swig from his mug of tea. "A big operation then. Is it possible that these came from another shipment, not one intended for the shop Riley manages?"

"In that case it's a huge coincidence that they turn up here."

Calladine nodded. She was right. "We need a word with Mr Riley and another go at Killian Seddon. If the theft of these things is down to Barton, one of the estate kids will know about it."

"He's trying hard to come over as all innocent and reformed, but that young man knows more than he's letting on." Ruth nodded at Calladine's mug. "That looks cold. Have you eaten?"

He sighed. "My usual allowance of salad and wholemeal bread."

"I'm disappointed in Killian," Ruth admitted. "I thought he'd turned a corner. Now I find out he's flogging bent gear around town and is possibly involved in murder."

"How d'you think I feel? I'm supposed to be painting scenery with him any day soon. He thinks we're on our way to being best buddies."

"Who do we tackle first?" she asked.

"We visit the Seddon flat and then out to the retail park to speak to Riley."

They were about to leave the office when Calladine's mobile rang. It was Natasha.

"Post-mortem first thing Monday morning. Unfortunately, today is out of the question as I'm in court."

Calladine was secretly dreading this one. The older he got, the more brutality he saw, the less he could stomach it. "We'll be there," he said.

They went into the main office. "Alice, do a check on any local warehouse robberies there've been in recent weeks. If you can't find anything, ask about rumours. Then see what you can find out about one Robin Riley, manager of the Northern Sportswear store on the retail park. If you get anything interesting, let me know at once."

He nodded at Rocco. "Close the door, this is for the team only."

Calladine saw the expectant looks and wished he had something more positive to tell them. "We've learned that the trainers, whether they be genuine or fake, are not on general sale yet. The stores are waiting for the distributors to give them the nod. I want this information keeping between ourselves for now. I'm not sure how this will help, but it's possible that whoever stole them isn't aware of it."

"You think the trainers and stuff was got from a robbery?" Ruth asked when they were out of the room.

"If they're genuine, I don't see how else they could have been. Our prime suspect for the theft is Barton, but we've no proof," Calladine said.

"But if the theft hasn't been reported, pointing the finger at anyone will be difficult. D'you think Riley is involved? He's reluctant to admit that anything's wrong, according to Kitty, but he has to be aware of what's going on. He'll be stock down for a start," Ruth said.

"Let's see what Alice finds first."

* * *

Killian was at home with his mum but there was no sign of Dean.

Calladine took the box from under his arm and opened it. "Tell me about these. You've got a pair, I can see them on your feet. Where did yours come from?"

"They're only poxy trainers, why d'you want to know?"

"They're hardly that, Killian," Ruth said. "They're expensive, designer trainers and way out of your league. So come on, who sold them to you?"

"Noah."

"Who supplied him?" Calladine asked.

"How should I know?"

"Is your Dean involved in this?"

Killian glared at Calladine. "Involved in what? I've done nowt, just bought a pair of trainers off a friend. Dean knew Noah was selling them and he knew they were dodgy. Problem was, dodgy or not, Dean couldn't afford them."

"I want to know where Noah got them from," Calladine insisted. "I reckon you know very well who's behind this scam."

"Look, a market trader, Knowles, he was selling them. Noah knew him. From time to time Noah got him stuff, and when Knowles had anything interesting he'd give Noah a shout. That's all there is to it."

"Did Knowles supply anyone other than Noah?" Calladine asked.

Killian shook his head vigorously. "How should I know? Knowles had a market stall, he could have been selling them on there for weeks."

"Did you know Rob Knowles?" Calladine asked.

"Everyone knows him. He's the 'go to' bloke if you need sommat."

"Have you heard any rumours on the estate about the trainers, Killian?" Ruth asked. "Anything, no matter how unimportant you think it is."

The lad hung his head. "I'm no grass. I tell you things and I get my head kicked in."

"Not telling us could get you into even more bother. Knowles has been murdered and we're looking for his killer."

His mother went pale. She moved to her son's side, grabbed his arm and shook him. "Tell 'em, son. You don't want to go down for murder, not to save that scally's arse."

"Which scally do you mean, Mrs Seddon?" Calladine asked.

"Barton, that's who."

CHAPTER TWENTY-TWO

Who next, Riley or Luke Barton?" Ruth asked once they were back in the car.

"Barton. At some stage we'll have to speak to Knowles's wife, ask if she knew what was going on, but we'll leave her for now. Let's see what Barton's got to say for himself."

"At this time of day he'll be at work, Goddard's Garden Centre."

"It's hardly surprising we got Barton's name out of Killian. He features heavily in all aspects of this case."

"This chain is getting longer, Tom. Noah, Barton and then back to Knowles. What we need to know is where that stock originated, who stole it in the first place."

"That could have been Barton, he did work at the Northern store for a short while. Check with Alice, see if we have anything on him."

"We don't, we've already checked, remember, but there are plenty of rumours."

"Speak to her again, see if any of the rumours fit. Barton or not, someone got hold of those trainers. Despite what Riley told Kitty, they didn't just fly into Knowles's lock-up."

"D'you think Noah was murdered because of them? Because if he was, why the mark incised in his flesh, and what about the attack on Barton, what's that all about?" Ruth asked.

"If we're ruling out something from the past, then given Barton and Spooner's animosity towards each other, it makes sense for Spooner to be his attacker."

"But if Spooner attacked Barton it follows that he could have attacked and killed Noah, both had the mark."

Calladine's head was spinning with facts, old and new. Names, motives, and memories of that old case. "I don't know what to think. The killings of Noah and Knowles are very different. Noah wasn't shot in the head for a start. If it wasn't for the connection with the trainers, there's no way we'd link them."

Ruth nodded. He was right. "Perhaps there isn't a link and the trainers are simply a coincidence."

"I don't go much on coincidence. Noah was involved in this scam, he was selling trainers to local lads. Either Barton or Knowles may or may not have been supplying him, and now both he and Knowles are dead. There has to be a link between the killings," Calladine said.

Ruth pulled into the car park at Goddard's. "I'll speak to Alice before we tackle Barton, see if she's got anything useful."

Alice had been busy. She'd not found out anything more about Spooner, Barton or Knowles, and the Shadow case file would take weeks to plod through. But she had discovered something interesting about the watch found on Noah's wrist.

"It's like the trainers and the bags, sir, expensive, high end and sold only in a small number of stores. It retails at a small fortune. The man I spoke to at the jewellers in town said that particular model was one of a batch that had been stolen recently, a particularly violent robbery of a container load of jewellery in the Midlands. The driver was killed."

"He's sure about that?" Calladine asked.

"Yes, I sent him photos, the serial number, the lot. He was quite certain. He can't understand how that particular watch came to be found on Noah's body."

"Good work, Alice. See what else you can find out."

Calladine wasn't sure what to make of it but it had to be significant. He told Ruth what Alice had discovered and asked what she thought.

"I'm as puzzled as you. We've got trainers that haven't yet hit the shops and now watches that are part of a violent robbery. Then there's the bags. I wonder what their pedigree is?"

"Alice is still researching. Knowing where the stuff originally came from would help."

"It's no good speculating, we need more info. But I don't understand why if the trainers were stolen, it hasn't been reported. The other stuff was."

"It'll be down to some scam or other, possibly involving Riley. Anyway, let's get on with the job in hand."

"Busy place this," Ruth noted. "And the café's full. The business must take a small fortune over the course of a week."

"Barton's just one of the workers not the owner, so profits or not, they won't go into his wallet."

"Back again." It was Marcus Goddard, walking towards them, a big smile on his face.

"We're after Barton," Calladine told him.

"Sorry, he's not turned up. Hence me in this overall doing his job."

"Did he ring, make an excuse?" Ruth asked.

"No, and he knows the rules."

"Has he been ill? Have you any idea what's going on with him?" she said.

Goddard shrugged. "I'm his employer, not his mate. We're too busy here for much chit-chat during the day. He was in yesterday, he seemed normal enough to me."

"What do these want?" A female voice rang out.

It was Lena Goddard, Marcus's mother, wife of Mark, the man Calladine had helped put away for a long time.

"You're not welcome here, so go on, get lost. My working day is arduous enough without having to look at your face."

Charming as ever. Calladine smiled at the woman. "Sorry, Lena, but I have no choice. We're investigating a murder and the trail has led us here."

Lena Goddard was in her fifties, slim, blonde, with strong features that gave her face a hard look. Hands on hips, she strode up to Calladine. "Then go and investigate somewhere else. There's nothing for you here. And if you continue to worry my staff, I'll have you thrown off the premises."

"Luke Barton. Know him?"

She glared at Calladine and nodded. "What's he done?"

"Not sure yet, but I need a word urgently."

"He lives on that damned estate, look there 'cause he's not here."

This was a waste of time. "If he turns up," Calladine said, "tell him we called and I still want that word."

The pair walked back to the car. "She really doesn't like you, does she? Did you see the look? Sheer hate." Ruth shuddered. "I reckon Lena Goddard is trouble."

"She's calmed down a lot since Mark was banged up. That clipped her wings good and proper."

"I had a quick glance at the file. Suspicion was that Lena was every bit as involved in Mark's activities as him."

"True, but we couldn't prove it. I reckoned then that Lena was as much the brains behind the operation as Mark. Every robbery, every scam was meticulously planned. Mark was no planner, believe me, too hot-headed. Lena was on holiday with her mother when Mark took over, and his sloppiness got him caught. I suspect that Mark decided the robbery was too good to miss and went for it without Lena's input. It was a mistake and his undoing."

"But you can't prove that."

"No, and it irritated the hell out of me at the time. Still does. That woman deserves to be behind bars every bit as much as her husband."

CHAPTER TWENTY-THREE

The next stop was Northern Sportswear on the Retail Park off the Ring Road.

Ruth parked the car and the pair sat for several minutes looking at the premises. "It's huge," Ruth said. "And Riley manages this lot. It must keep him busy."

"Whoever Northern Sportswear are, they've made a huge investment. Wonder where the money came from."

"The bank, I'd imagine. Sportswear is very popular so a good bet," she said.

"C'mon then, let's get Riley's take on this," Calladine said.

"What I don't understand is how come there's nothing missing. I'd say there had to be, but why lie?"

Ruth had a point but trying to work it out made Calladine's head hurt. He was hoping that there'd been some mistake and sometime soon Riley would realise that he was stock down. If not, then it begged the question, was he part of this?

Robin Riley was in his office, a large space at the rear of the shop area given over to administering this arm of the enterprise.

"What can I do for you?" he asked after they'd introduced themselves.

"Kitty Lake," Calladine began. "She spoke to you about certain items of your stock that's not yet on sale but is currently being traded on the streets of Leesworth."

Blunt and to the point. Riley looked rattled. He looked around furtively and whispered, "I don't want this getting out, so please keep your voices down. Miss Lake came here and I told her everything I knew, but I specifically asked her to be discreet. I do not want all and sundry knowing about the stock, it won't go down well with senior management."

"We're not all and sundry, Mr Riley, we're the police," Calladine said.

Riley nodded. "It's important that both the suppliers and the board of Northern Sportswear have confidence in my operation here. If the area manager, James Halpin, were to find out about the missing stock there'd be hell to pay. You see I have already taken delivery of our share of the stock. I've got it locked away in the stockroom at the back of the building. Halpin gets wind of this and I'll get the blame." He checked to ensure no one was listening. "Please tell me you haven't told anyone that the trainers are not on general release yet. That will only make those stray pairs all the more desirable."

"No, that information is restricted to my team, Miss Lake and yourselves."

Riley nodded. "Good. The advertising campaign is due to go live and head office would be livid if they thought even the possibility of a new design had been leaked."

"Your missing stock is linked to two murders we're currently investigating, hence our interest," Calladine said.

"Murders!" Riley echoed. "And it involves the trainers? I'm at a loss. In the unlikely event that stock did go missing from here I've no idea whose hands they ended up in."

"What's the schedule for their release?" Ruth asked.

"They will go on sale across the country on a specific date. If management discover that stock is available here in Leesdon before that date they won't be happy. A fortune is earmarked for advertising. Word gets out beforehand and they'll blame me, bound to, and I can't vouch for what will happen to me or the staff here. I expect the board will insist we all get our marching orders."

"Did Miss Lake's investigation throw up anything helpful?" Calladine asked.

"No, the entire thing was a waste of time. She got nothing, but still presented me with a hefty bill."

Calladine knew that wasn't true. Kitty had discovered that Knowles was selling them on his market stall and intended to interview him. She'd also spoken to Killian Seddon.

"Are you sure there's no stock missing?" he asked.

"No, it's all present and correct."

"But that doesn't make sense, Mr Riley," Calladine said.

"Granted what I've seen on the feet of several youngsters look the business, but if you're telling the truth they've got to be fakes, that's the only explanation."

Riley seemed certain enough but was he right? He hadn't even asked about the murders either, not even who the victims were. "They look pretty authentic to us," Calladine said. "But we're no experts."

"I had my staff doing a stock-check last weekend just to make absolutely sure that all is as it should be."

"When do they go on sale in the shops?" Ruth asked.

"It's still to be decided, but the advertising starts in a week. On the back of that we expect pre-orders to be excellent."

Calladine was surprised. In his opinion the trainers were too pricy to be overly popular. "Could we take a look at your warehouse, see where the stock is kept?"

Riley didn't look too happy with the idea but nevertheless he led the way to the rear of the store. Taking a set of keys from his jacket pocket, he led them down a corridor and outside to a building in the yard. "Bars on the windows, and top of the range locks," he said. He let them in, switched on the lights and stood to one side. "See, box after box of our new line. All have been counted and all are present and correct."

Calladine walked along the middle aisle between the racks of shelving. He looked closely at the boxes and the labels. "Mind if I open one?" he asked.

Riley pulled a face. "Yes, I do. I have a meeting in Huddersfield in less than an hour."

"But you checked inside the boxes when you did the stock-take?"

"I really must insist. The meeting is important and I can't be late."

His reluctance spoke volumes. "Luke Barton worked for you. What was he like?"

"A waste of space and totally untrustworthy. I caught him myself trying to leave one night with a bag full of T-shirts. I sacked him on the spot."

"Could he have stolen the trainers?"

That flustered Riley. He looked at his watch and tutted. "I really do have to leave now."

Calladine handed Riley a card. "Okay, should anything change, ring me."

"What d'you think?" Calladine asked once he and Ruth were out of the store.

"I'm not sure. He didn't like the question about Barton. If you ask me, that young scally stole the trainers and Riley knows it."

"He knows damn well there's stock missing. He counted boxes, Ruth, that's not checking stock."

"He certainly didn't want you delving too closely. He could be part of whatever's going on," Ruth suggested. "Perhaps Barton was leaning on him. He can be pretty scary."

"If we're not careful we'll end up thinking everyone in this case is being leaned on. But why and by who?"

The only thing that made any sense was that Barton had stolen the trainers, or that he and Riley were fiddling the system, hiving off stock and passing it to the likes of Knowles to sell on. But if that was the case, why hire Kitty? The man had some nerve to face the police with such certainty that there'd been no theft. Double bluff perhaps?

"Another word with Kitty and then that chat with Spooner. He still owes us."

Ruth checked the time on her mobile. "It's getting on. Kitty will have locked up and gone home by now."

Calladine was already tapping out a text. "We're in luck, she's at mine. We'll have that chat and a bite to eat at the same time."

"It's my day for picking up Harry from nursery. Jake has his advanced literature class after school."

"Okay, I'll speak to Kitty myself and then deal with Spooner."

"And tomorrow it's Saturday, or had you forgotten?"

"It makes no difference to me."

But it did to Ruth. "I have a family, Tom. Jake understands about my job, he really does, but he also likes us to spend at least some of the weekend together."

She was right. He wouldn't mind spending some time with Zoe and the baby either.

"Okay you get off. I'll give you a ring, bring you up to speed when I've done. No sense in both of us getting bogged down with the case."

CHAPTER TWENTY-FOUR

But Kitty was in no mood to talk. "Look, Tom, I've had a busy day and all I want to do is forget work, have a bite to eat and put my feet up if it's all the same to you."

Calladine would have liked nothing better than to join her but he had two murders to solve and Kitty could help.

"Two people have been murdered, a young lad and Rob Knowles," he said grimly. "I have to find out who killed them and why."

"I seriously doubt I can help much."

Ignoring the comment, Calladine asked, "Riley — what did you make of him?"

Kitty flopped onto the sofa and retrieved a notebook from her bag. After consulting her notes, she said, "He contacted me a week ago. He'd seen several youngsters in Leesdon wearing trainers about to go on sale in the five Northern Sportswear stores. He told me he'd checked the stock in his branch himself and insisted that nothing was missing. I asked Riley the usual stuff — was he sure about the stock, there hadn't been some mistake had there, but he was adamant." Kitty shook her head. "I was confused. I'd seen for myself any number of kids around town wearing them. I spoke to Killian Seddon, as you know, and he said he got them from Rob Knowles. Knowles was murdered before I could speak to him."

That all sounded straightforward enough. "Is there anything else in that little book of yours?"

Kitty was silent while she deciphered her scrawl. "It might be nothing, but it was something Killian said."

"Go on."

"He's got some mouth on him, every second word's an expletive, and he was guarded about what he told me. But he got angry at one point, it was when I asked if I could buy his trainers off him. I was going to get them checked out, make sure they were genuine. He went all red, told me to bugger off and bother someone else. Said there was more going on than just trainers and hadn't I come across the bags or watches yet."

"Bags and watches? You're sure that's what he said?"

"Yes, he has a short fuse, got all het up and stormed off, but that was the gist of it."

"We found a number of designer handbags in Knowles's lock-up and Noah Crosby had an expensive gold watch on his wrist when we found his body."

Kitty shivered. "A young lad like that, lying dead in an alleyway for weeks on end. I don't know how you do the job, Tom."

"Me neither, love. And the longer I do it, the harder it gets."

Calladine disappeared into the small dining room to look at his files. What Kitty had told him made sense from what they already knew, but it also meant that there had to be other retailers involved, apart from those managed by Riley. The stores selling the bags and watches for starters. Killian Seddon obviously knew more than he'd told him and Ruth. He'd put that right in the morning.

He could hear his mobile trill, he'd left it on the coffee table in the sitting room. "Get that for me, would you?" he called to Kitty.

Moments later, she walked into the dining room, stuck it in his face before walking away and slamming the door behind her. Calladine saw the name on the screen and understood why — Amy.

"She is one unfriendly woman," were her first words. "Not the sort of person you need around you, Tom."

"What d'you want?"

"Now now. I'm family these days, remember. I shouldn't need an excuse to ring you."

"I'm busy, Amy, and I don't have time to play games."

"No game. Julian and I want you to come round tomorrow afternoon and see Maisie. Zoe and Jo are having the day to themselves and I thought you'd enjoy spending time with the little one." She paused, no doubt giving him time to mull this over. "We could walk by the canal, feed the ducks and then have tea in that nice little café."

Calladine sighed. Why did life have to be so damned difficult? Of course he wanted to go, but what about Kitty?

"What's wrong? You've gone all quiet. Worried your girlfriend won't approve? Well, I've got the solution for that — ask her to come along."

"You'll behave?"

"I'm a grown woman and well over you, Tom Calladine. Of course I'll behave. Come round to Julian's at about two, it's forecast to be sunny and warm. We'll have a nice time, take some photos and make some memories."

"Okay, see you tomorrow then."

All he had to do now was convince Kitty that this was all above board and not Amy playing games.

But when he went to tell her, she said, "She wants you back. Whatever she says, it's all part of her plan."

"Planning isn't something Amy does much," Calladine said. "She's a spur of the moment, instinctive kind of woman. Anyway, I doubt she'd have me back."

"Don't you believe it. She's got her claws out, I know the signs. What did she want? To entertain you this weekend? Lure you in with the promise of seeing little Maisie, did she?"

"She's invited both you and me to feed the ducks and then go for a cuppa at that café by the canal. And, yes, it's about me seeing Maisie, but what's wrong with that?"

Kitty rolled her eyes. "You said yes, of course."

Calladine nodded. "I said you'd come too."

"Okay, but mark my words, Amy is up to something and it won't end well."

CHAPTER TWENTY FIVE

Saturday

First thing Saturday morning, Calladine rang Rocco and asked him to meet him at the Seddons' place on the Hobfield.

"Young Killian's not been altogether honest with us," he said. "He knows a lot more than he's told us about the gear Knowles was selling."

"How do we play it? Want to take him down the station?"

Calladine nodded. "If he refuses to answer or gets edgy in any way, yes. A little time spent in the cells might make him see sense. I don't know him well but I get the impression the lad's not bad, just easily led."

Killian's mother answered the door in her dressing gown, peered warily up and down the street and then beckoned them inside. "It's the weekend, don't you lot ever give it a rest?"

"A word with Killian," Calladine said.

She gave a furtive glance up the staircase. "He's not here."

"Mind if we look?"

"Look where you like but you won't find him."

Calladine nodded to Rocco. "Why the nerves this morning? Is it Killian?"

She pulled the dressing gown tighter round her slim body. "Everything's fine. Killian'll be back soon, I've no need to be nervous of anything, I've got my boys for protection."

"Protection from what, Mrs Seddon?" he asked.

"He's not here, sir," Rocco called out. "And his bed's not been slept in."

"Where is he?" Calladine asked.

She burst into tears. "The truth is, I don't know. I've not slept a wink. He got a call last night, went out and that's the last I saw of him."

"D'you know who the call was from?"

She shook her head.

"What time was this?"

"About nine. He said he wouldn't be long so I waited up. After he'd been gone a couple of hours I rang him but his mobile was dead. Dean went out to look for him, he spoke to a few of the lads but no one had seen him."

"Is there anywhere he'd go? To a friend's house, perhaps?"

"He hangs about with Dean and before he got killed, Noah. I don't like him hanging out with the estate lads, they're trouble."

Calladine was concerned. Killian knew about the missing stock, which meant he was involved. He might also be involved with those who took it. That put him perilously close to whoever killed Knowles and Noah.

"Where's Dean now?" Calladine asked.

"The lad's still in bed," Rocco confirmed.

"Get him up," Calladine said to his mother. "I need a word with him."

Ten minutes later, a tousled-headed Dean yawned his way down the stairs. "Look, I don't know what our Killian's up to, but if I were him I'd be steering well clear of Barton and his mob."

"What makes you say that?" Calladine asked. "Why would Barton intimidate Killian?"

"'Cause he's got a loose mouth, can't keep it shut."

"Are you talking about the trainers and other stuff?" Calladine asked.

Dean nodded. "He should have stayed well away but he's an idiot, just like Noah. Well perhaps not an idiot, but he's far too easily led and he doesn't see any harm in people. That can get you into big trouble round here. Knowles took advantage. He wanted him to ask around, see if any of the kids were interested in buying the trainers from him at a special price. Barton got wind of it and got angry."

"Why should the goods Knowles sold upset Barton?"

"No good asking me. Perhaps he wanted in. When he wants something, he gets it. Stand in his way and he can be a vicious sod."

Dean was telling the truth. The sharp tongued, street wise kid was gone, to be replaced by a lad genuinely concerned for his brother.

"I'm going to ask a uniformed officer to call round and take a formal statement from you, Dean. You simply tell him everything you've told me," Calladine said.

"He'll get his head ripped off if he does that," his mother interposed.

"The officer who comes here will stay and keep an eye on things. Your home will be watched round the clock until I'm happy that there's no more danger."

CHAPTER TWENTY-SIX

Calladine rang the station and organised an officer to take a statement from Dean and keep a watch on the house. He also issued orders for Luke Barton to be found and brought in.

"The garden centre?" Rocco asked.

"Shortly, but first we'll make sure Barton's not at home. He only lives a few doors up," Calladine said.

Irene Barton took one look at the pair and was about to slam the door shut when Rocco put his foot against it.

"Why so unfriendly? All we want is a word with Luke," Calladine said.

She confronted them, her face red with fury. "He's not here. You should know. You lot came round last night and carted him off. Not even a phone call and I'm sure that's not right. I want him back and quick. He's got a doctor's appointment this morning with his arm."

Calladine frowned, puzzled. As far as he was aware Barton hadn't been taken to the station. "Give the nick a ring," he told Rocco. "Find out what happened."

"It shouldn't be allowed. We were just having tea in front of the telly when you lot came banging at the door and screaming. The big bloke said he'd be home within the hour, so where is he?"

"I'll sort it, Mrs Barton," Calladine said.

Phone at his ear, Rocco beckoned from the doorway. "We've not got him, sir," he whispered. "Neither has Oldston."

Now what was going on? Calladine turned back to Barton's mother. "The officer who took Luke away, did you get his name?"

"No, he were some big burly bloke, in plain clothes like you though not a suit. I didn't know him, I don't think he was local."

Calladine and Rocco left Mrs Barton glaring at them from her doorway. "Goddard's," Calladine said. "And let's hope he's there."

"If he's not?"

"Then I haven't a clue where to look."

* * *

The two drove the short distance to the garden centre, only to find the main gates locked.

"Shut, but it's the weekend, the place should be heaving," Rocco said. "What d'you reckon's happened?"

"Could be anything, but I hope it's nothing to do with Barton." Calladine took out his mobile and called them.

Marcus Goddard answered.

"Why aren't you open?" Calladine asked.

"No need to be concerned, Inspector." Marcus sounded amused. "We're stocktaking this morning. Things will be back to normal this afternoon. You can pop in and look at the perennials then."

Ignoring the sarcasm, Calladine said, "I want a word with Luke Barton, is he with you?"

"No. He wasn't in yesterday and he was absent again this morning. Still not rung in either, so I've no idea what's going on. Hopefully we'll see him later today."

"When did you last see him?" Calladine asked.

"Earlier in the week. To be fair, he's not someone I take much notice of. So long as he does the work, then it's fine by me."

"And you haven't heard from him at all?" Calladine asked.

"What is this?" Marcus laughed. "I don't keep tabs on my staff every hour of the day."

"Barton turns up later, you ring me," Calladine told him.

"Of course, only too pleased to help the police." Marcus's tone was beginning to irritate Calladine.

"Where to now?" Rocco asked.

Calladine handed over the keys and climbed into the passenger seat. "You drive. Next on the list is the Spooner place."

"Given it wasn't us arrested Barton last night, where d'you reckon he's got to?" Rocco asked.

Good question but Calladine had no idea. What he did have was a horrible feeling that Barton had met the same fate as Knowles. Another worry — where did the 'burly bloke' his mother had spoken of fit into this damned puzzle?

* * *

Ricky Spooner was at home, he seemed quiet, subdued and distracted. He spent most of their conversation staring out of the sitting room window at the road outside.

"Are you expecting someone?" Calladine finally asked. "Only you've barely taken your eyes off that road."

"An important delivery," Spooner said. "Don't want to miss it."

"We've been through this before, but this time I want the truth," Calladine began. "Tell me about your relationship with Noah Crosby and Luke Barton."

"Don't give up, do you, copper? I'm not a liar. Everything I've said has been the truth."

"It's honesty or the station, Ricky. The choice is yours."

"Okay," he conceded. "This is all I know. Noah was nothing but a daft kid. He ran errands for me occasionally, cleaned cars at the showroom for a few quid." He spread his hands. "There you are, that's it. There's nothing more to tell."

"And Barton?"

"I don't have anything to do with Barton, he's bad news so word has it."

"Word has it that the pair of you have locked horns over the Hobfield, and which one of you's going to supply the punters with what they need."

With a laugh, Spooner got up and closed the sitting room door. "I'd prefer it if my mother wasn't privy to your ridiculous accusations."

"You were stopped by an officer, your bag was searched and a number of pairs of trainers were found. Care to explain?"

"Not really, Mr Calladine. I can barely recall the incident. Apart from which, I'm sure whoever stopped me must have been mistaken about what they saw. I'm not interested in trainers." He smiled.

"When did you last see Noah Crosby?" Calladine asked again.

"Can't recall. Truth be told, I was never that interested in the lad."

They were getting nowhere. They'd no real proof that Spooner had had anything to do with Noah at all, only hearsay. Calladine was about to call time on the interview when he noticed what Spooner was wearing on his wrist. Finally, the possible break they so badly needed. Things could be looking up at last.

"Nice watch. Where'd you get it from?"

"It was a birthday present from my mother."

"When was that?" Rocco asked.

"Why? Going to put it your diary, Detective, so you don't miss sending me a card? Spooner held out his arm to show them. "Two months since. Why the interest?"

"Watches matching that particular design are on a list of property we're interested in. I'd like to know who your mother bought it from."

Spooner's face fell. "She didn't buy it. She gave me the money and I bought it from a friend. He needed some cash urgently, I liked the watch so we cut a deal. I didn't realise the thing was hot."

Calladine smiled. "I don't know that it is. But it could be linked to our murder investigation. I think you should come down to the station with us. We need to have a proper chat."

CHAPTER TWENTY-SEVEN

Ricky Spooner sat quietly in the cell waiting for his solicitor to arrive. He'd been processed, required to empty his pockets and hand his belongings, including the gold watch, to the desk sergeant.

"What's going on here?" Calladine asked Rocco, turning the watch over in his hands. "Worth a bob or two, stolen d'you think? Noah Crosby was wearing an identical one when he was found. What have we stumbled on?"

"A racket of some sort."

Calladine nodded. Rocco had to be right, but how did it work and who was behind it? He doubted it was Spooner. "The trainers aren't officially missing. The watches and bags could be another matter. What's going on? Whoever is running this scam, how do they get hold of this stuff?"

"You think Spooner knows?" Rocco asked. "I find that very unlikely. He doesn't strike me as being the brains behind anything."

"He knows something. A small cog perhaps, but what he knows could be the key to cracking this case."

"His brief's arrived," said a uniformed officer.

Calladine made for the door. "Right, let's go and see what he's got to say for himself."

Spooner's solicitor, Clive Collymore, was from a high profile firm in Manchester. Sitting safely in his shadow, Ricky Spooner must be thinking he held all the cards and the interview would be a breeze.

"The gold watch, Ricky. Where did you get it?" Calladine began.

He shrugged. "Can't tell you."

"If you want to get out of here any time soon, you will have to."

"My client has explained to me about the watch and the trainers, Inspector. He came by the watch innocently," the solicitor said. "As for the trainers, your officer was mistaken so what you've got is one man's word against the other."

"In that case he won't mind telling me how the watch came to be in his possession," Calladine said.

Spooner sighed. "I promised not to say anything. That watch was supposed to be a present for his wife."

"I'm losing patience, just get on with it."

"An old friend of mine came into the garage," Spooner began. "He'd seen a car he liked but couldn't meet the price. We did a deal, simple as that. He paid over the cash and made up the difference with the watch. He said he'd come in the near future to buy it back. See, Inspector, no mystery, just business."

"Does this customer, this *old friend*, have a name?" Rocco asked.

"Rob Knowles," Spooner said.

"You're lying," Calladine said at once. Spooner wasn't taking this seriously and it irritated him. "No way could Knowles afford a watch like the one you have, and I seriously doubt he'd be an old friend of yours. Before his brutal murder, Knowles was a market trader fighting for every penny."

"I know what he was, but once in a while he had some proper gems for sale, quite literally." Spooner grinned.

"Do you know where he got the watch from?" Calladine asked.

"I didn't ask. He wanted to trade and I wanted the watch. He assured me that he'd come by it honestly and I believed him."

"It's a very pricy watch, Ricky, weren't you curious?"

"Doesn't do to ask too many questions. We did the deal and that was that."

Calladine had serious reservations, but he could neither prove nor disprove Spooner's tale. "Have you seen Luke Barton lately?"

Spooner had sailed through the questions about the watch without a flicker but this one made him look suddenly nervous. "Why d'you ask?"

"He seems to have disappeared, young Killian Seddon too."

"I don't mix with either of them. They both come from that dump of an estate, and I prefer to keep well away."

His words were too glib, like they'd been well practised. "Come on now, Ricky, you know the Hobfield well enough. I've heard the rumours. You have a reputation, the kids know you. You're the one they run to when they're after drugs."

"That's not true!" he shouted, rising to his feet. "I don't deal drugs and I never have. Whoever is spreading this rubbish is lying."

Collymore cleared his throat. "D'you have any evidence to support these accusations, Inspector? Either about the drug dealing or the murder of this man Knowles?"

Calladine shook his head and then said, "no" for the tape. He had nothing, he'd been hoping that Spooner would give something away under pressure but that hadn't happened.

"This is going nowhere," the solicitor said. "You have nothing concrete on my client, and therefore you must release him without charge."

He was right but it still turned Calladine's stomach. "Don't disappear," he said to Spooner. "I'll probably need to speak to you again."

The pair left the room while Calladine gathered together his paperwork. "What's your take on Spooner?" he asked Rocco.

"He was pretty sure about the dealing. He was quite emphatic about it having nothing to do with him."

"Yes, but they're all like that."

Rocco didn't look so sure. "I hate to say it, sir, but I believed him. I reckon that whatever Spooner's involved in on the Hobfield, it's not drugs."

"And Barton?"

"He's a different matter — streetwise, canny, and constantly on his guard. He could be up to anything," Rocco said.

Calladine checked the time. "I've got a date this afternoon with the family."

"Look, you get off, sir. I'm not in any hurry to finish. Alice is up to her ears in research for the case. While she works I'll take another trip round to Goddard's and see if Barton's turned up."

"Don't go alone, be sure to take a uniform with you."

CHAPTER TWENTY EIGHT

Calladine went home to change and found a note from Kitty waiting for him. She'd cried off. Apparently, she had to meet someone in Oldston about a case and wouldn't be back in time. More than likely it was an excuse. Well, he might have expected it.

Amy was right, the weather was glorious and deserved to be made the most of. Dressed in a pair of light-coloured slacks and a short sleeved shirt, he made his way on foot to Julian's apartment. The block was in a lovely spot overlooking the canal, with a hillside beyond. During the walk he mulled things over. It was time to be honest with himself, admit he was finding life with Kitty hard going. Amy was a delight by comparison.

"What d'you think of Maisie's new frock, grandaddy?" Amy was holding the infant up, a big grin on her face. "We've been shopping. There's a lovely baby boutique on the High Street, I can see us girls spending a lot of time in there."

Smiling, Calladine took the bundle from her. Maisie gave a little gurgle, yawned, and snuggled into his shoulder.

"Busy morning. We'll have a walk, give her time for a nap and then it's the ducks and tea."

"Kitty's got work," he said. "She sends her apologies."

Amy laughed. "I'd have been more surprised if she had turned up. Kitty's afraid that I'll steal you right from under her eyes and she's given up without a fight. The woman is supposed to love you, so what's she up to?"

"She's working. Life's tough in her line, so give her a break."

Amy pulled a face, took Maisie from his arms and set her down in the pram. "Let's go while the sun's still shining." She thrust a bag of duck food into his hands. "Here, carry this."

He smiled. "Bread not good enough these days?"

"It's bad for them, upsets their tummies, and we don't want that."

They left the apartment, went down the lift, round to the back entrance and out onto the canal bank. "We'll wander this way," Amy said, pointing. "She likes to see the other kids in the park up here."

"It didn't take you long to learn the ropes."

"I think this is great. Julian has given me something I never expected, a foot in the future. I want to be part of Maisie's life and intend to spend as much time as I can with her."

"Wish I could do the same, but work . . . you know what I'm going to say."

"Then give it up, take that leap and retire while you're still fit and able to enjoy it."

Not something he wanted to think too deeply about. "Don't start. I love my granddaughter but I'm not ready to ditch the job just yet."

The park was situated at the rear of the museum. They were about to turn towards the swings when someone called out to him. "Tom!"

Calladine turned to see Eve Buckley, his mother, waving at him.

"Why is it that I have to either bump into you by accident or by dint of the job, otherwise months go by without so much as a phone call."

"Sorry. Lot on," he mumbled.

"Amy, good to see you." Eve nodded towards the building. "Museum business. It's never-ending and invariably at the weekend, given the people who run it have jobs in the week. Speaking of your job, Tom, any closer to finding who killed poor Rob Knowles? His wife is terribly distressed about it. Blames herself, so her sister told me."

That sparked Calladine's curiosity. "Why?"

"Apparently, she was constantly warning him about the company he kept and the stock he was selling. From what little I've learned, his stock wasn't always acquired legitimately."

"That much I know, what I don't know is who is behind getting him that stock."

"Youngsters, according to Brenda. A couple of them collared Rob at his market stall a couple of weeks back trying to thrust more stock on him. Rob didn't want it and there was a shouting match. It got so heated another stall holder was on the brink of calling you lot."

"How is Brenda? Up to speaking to me?" he asked.

"I'm sure she won't mind. I can ring her if you like, tell her to expect you."

"I'll collect some photos from the nick and get round there. Get it arranged will you, Eve?"

"I want something in return," she said. "You at mine for a meal tomorrow. I fancy a nice family Sunday afternoon. Why don't you come too, Amy? You can tell me all about Cornwall."

The prospect filled Calladine with dread. Making small talk with his half siblings was not his idea of how to spend a Sunday. And Eve appeared to have completely forgotten about Kitty. "I'll have to ring you on that one, Eve. The demands of the case, I'm sure you understand."

"Thanks for the invite," Amy said graciously. She turned to Tom. "You're not really going back to work, are you? What happened to our afternoon with the little one?"

At the mention of the child, Eve peered into the pram. "She's gorgeous, Tom. She makes me so proud." She beamed at Amy. "My first great-grandchild."

"I wish he was so enthusiastic," Amy said.

"Look, you two," he said, "I've got a killer to find and family or not, that has to take preference." He gave Eve a quick peck on the cheek. "I'll ring you about tomorrow. Amy, let me sort this and then I'll be back."

CHAPTER TWENTY-NINE

Calladine went back to his cottage, picked up his car and made for the station. The main office was empty, except for two uniforms and Alice at her desk, head down and muttering to herself.

"It's a nice day. Don't spend it all in here," he said.

"I was just about to ring you," she said. "I've been looking at particular robberies in other areas."

"And you've found something interesting?"

"Yes, with photos too." She spread them out across her desk. They showed detailed images of the watches and the designer handbags. "Look familiar? As we know, these watches were en route from a wholesale jewellers in London to a depot in the north of England from where they were to be distributed to a number of different shops. The container was robbed at a service station and the driver left badly injured. As for the bags, they're an expensive designer brand and would have retailed for a small fortune. They were manufactured abroad, have never been on sale in the UK and haven't even been advertised here yet. The ferry landed at Dover. The container with the bags rolled off and was found, emptied of its contents, at a service station off the M1 south of Birmingham. The local police took a look at the CCTV but got nothing. The lorry driver tried to stop the thieves and got a beating for his trouble, plus a bullet to the back of the head."

Calladine had presumed the watches and bags were stolen property but he'd had no idea of the scale. "Anything on the trainers?"

"That design is new and again not on general sale yet. Stock has been despatched to several stores around the country, including the five belonging to Northern Sportswear but so far no one has reported anything missing."

Which was odd. Calladine knew very well they had to be stolen. Barton was looking more and more suspect. "Good work, Alice, well done. Continue this on Monday but call it a day now, you've done enough."

"I'm all right, sir. Rocco rang in half an hour ago. He's on his way back. He's been to Goddard's but there was no sign of Barton. He spoke to Marcus Goddard but he hadn't heard from him."

That begged the question of where Barton had got to. With the memory of what had been done to Knowles in his head, Calladine had a bad feeling. "When Rocco returns, the pair of you wrap up for the weekend," he said. "Get out in the nice weather before it turns."

"And you? I thought you had plans too."

"Something to see to first, a possible witness," he said. Without explaining, he disappeared into his office to collect a selection of images to take with him. It would be of enormous help if Brenda Knowles recognised any of them.

* * *

The Knowles family lived in a neat semi on the outskirts of Leesdon, close to Ruth and Jake. Eve had warned Brenda that he was coming and Calladine found her pottering in the front garden.

She was nervous. When she pointed her trowel at a bed of flowers, Calladine noted that her hand was shaking.

"Don't know why I bother with these," she said. "The slugs always get them. Doesn't seem to matter what I put down."

"Eve said you might be able to help me," he said gently. "I wonder if you'd take a look at some photos, see if you recognise anyone?"

She avoided the question. "D'you like gardening? I have to say, it's the only thing that keeps me sane these days." She turned away from him, removed her gloves, and threw the trowel into a bucket. "You're talking about the louts who made Rob's life a misery. I don't need photos, I'd know them anywhere. I've lived round here long enough to know all the troublemakers. That Barton lad were one and the older of them Seddon boys the other."

"Luke Barton and Killian Seddon?" Calladine fished out the images, nonetheless, and showed them to her. "You're sure?"

"Yes, I know them both from when I worked on dinners at the high school."

"Are you aware of any others in their little gang?"

"It was always that pair that bothered Rob at his stall. Always trying to sell him stuff. When it came to the selling it was always Barton that cut the deals, he told Rob that he could get a variety of stuff. I warned Rob, told him it sounded decidedly iffy, but he wouldn't listen. For a while Barton supplied him with loads of stock, but it was the trainers that changed everything. The manager from that sportswear store started asking questions, so Rob realised where they'd come from. Once he knew, all he wanted was to get rid of what he had and call it a day."

"Are you sure Barton was working alone in this? He wasn't in cahoots with Ricky Spooner for instance."

"I'm not stupid, Mr Calladine. I know Ricky Spooner well enough, and I'm telling you, as far as I'm aware he wasn't involved."

Calladine nodded and decided to check for himself before taking her word for it. As far as he was concerned,

Spooner was still a person of interest in this case. "Have you any idea where Barton got the stock from?"

"No, and neither did Rob. He always said it was better not to ask questions."

"Did you ever see anyone else with Barton? I'm thinking older blokes."

"No, and Rob never spoke of anyone."

"Thanks, Mrs Knowles, you've been a great help."

CHAPTER THIRTY

Calladine went back to the station. He wanted another trawl through the file before calling it a day. What he'd learned about Barton fitted what they knew and had been told, but he was beginning to doubt what part Spooner had played in it all.

Local gossip had the pair as sworn enemies, locked in a pitched battle for supremacy of the Hobfield. But looking through recent cases, the truth was that there'd been very little activity on either the drugs or gang warfare front. It seemed that an elaborate web of lies had been woven around the pair, but why? What did either of them have to gain from it?

The young men were vastly different. Spooner's background was privileged, whereas Barton had been dragged up on the Hobfield. Calladine was curious to know what had thrown their names together, made them out to be locked in conflict over running the Hobfield.

Alice had left for the day but her research notes were lying on her desk. Calladine had a quick flick through. The watches and bags were accounted for by the robberies, but not the trainers. That gave credence to his growing suspicion that procuring them might be down to local skulduggery. Barton was in the frame, he'd worked at Northern.

Calladine disappeared into his own office and fired up his computer. Spooner and Barton were one thing but he wanted to take a look at the database, see if anything was known about either Riley or his manager, Halpin, before he went any further.

He searched the police database first before resorting to others, but he could find nothing on either man. They were both clean.

He checked his mobile and saw a text from Amy. If he'd finally finished for the weekend, she and Maisie were at Julian's apartment waiting for him to join them for tea. Calladine smiled to himself. How could he refuse? But first, he needed to update Kitty. He rang her number but it went straight to voicemail. Was she ignoring his call? He wouldn't blame her. He collected his stuff and left the office.

* * *

"The little mite was jiggered after the outing, so I've put her down."

Calladine stared at the sleeping bundle in the crib. She was so small, so vulnerable-looking. He felt a sudden stab of fear for her safety. Instantly dismissing it as tiredness, he turned towards Amy. She'd looked after the infant for most of the day. What with that and preparing the food, she must be tired herself. "Can I help?" he asked.

"You've missed all the slog. Take a seat and get stuck in."

Calladine sat down at the dining table and cast his eyes over the array of sandwiches, savoury morsels and cakes set out before him. "You've gone to a lot of trouble."

"You didn't make the café, so I thought a DIY effort was merited, this being our first proper get together since my return. I invited Eve to join us but she cried off. When we spotted her she was off to pick up her daughter, Sam, from the airport. D'you see much of your siblings?"

"Not if it can be avoided." He picked up a sandwich, opened it to see what was inside and took a bite. "They've been brought up in their world and me in mine. And very different worlds they are too. For starters, we didn't have the money at our disposal that the Buckleys had. There was no posh school for me, I had to make do with the local comp."

"That shouldn't make a difference. Eve's your mother and she clearly misses having you in her life." Amy paused for a moment, considering her next words. "Have you ever thought about the sacrifice she made?"

"What sacrifice? Giving me up? That was her own decision."

"Didn't you ever wonder how she must have felt?"

"I knew nothing about it. I was in the dark about my true parentage for decades."

"But later on, as the years went by, she must have regretted what she'd done. She must have wanted to approach you, tell you how she felt, or explain why things were the way they were."

"That couldn't happen. Years ago my dad, Eve, and Freda Jean made an agreement. Eve knew the score."

"It must have hurt. I'm not a mother myself, but I can imagine the emotions. In fact, I can sense them when I'm with her."

"That's very fanciful."

"I'm a fanciful person, Tom. But it's the truth. There's a sadness to her that becomes acute when she's near you. You need to develop your sensitive side. You miss a lot."

Calladine had never had much time for Amy's mumbo-jumbo and chose to ignore the remark. "Grub's good," he said, pouring a cup of tea. "When's Zoe due back?"

"Any time. She doesn't like leaving Maisie for too long."

Calladine got to his feet. "Right then, tell her I'll ring later. I should be going. Still got work to do, stuff to look through at home."

"I bet that pleases Kitty. How does she cope with you?"

"I'm not sure she does. Kitty has been a bit on the cool side lately. I reckon she finds me heavy going."

"A quick learner."

Calladine leaned forward and kissed Amy's cheek. "Sorry about spoiling the day, but I will make it up to you."

"I doubt it. I know you of old, remember. Don't worry about my finer feelings, I've learned to cope."

He left the apartment and walked into what was left of the day's sunshine. He was crossing the park when someone called out to him.

"DI Calladine? Tom?"

It was DCI Stephen Greco, and he had a bloke with him that Calladine didn't know.

Greco introduced the man. "This is DI Jeff Dawlish, Midlands Serious Crime. Have you got time for a chat?"

CHAPTER THIRTY-ONE

Calladine put Jeff Dawlish at about his own age and shorter, with thinning brown hair that was greying at the edges. He was smartly dressed in a dark suit and white shirt with striped tie.

Calladine led the pair to a table outside the teashop by the canal. "What can I help you with?"

Dawlish handed him his warrant card. "First off, you'd better take a look at this, reassure yourself that I'm on the level."

Calladine smiled. "If DCI Greco vouches for you, that's good enough for me."

"The pair of you appear to be working the same case in different areas," Greco said. "Tom, I want you to give Jeff all the help you can, and I'm sure he'll reciprocate." With that he got up from the table, said his goodbyes and left them to it.

"Fancy a cuppa?" Calladine asked.

"I wouldn't say no. I could do with a bite to eat too, it's been a bit of a journey."

Calladine cleared his throat and gestured to the waitress. "Rare afternoon off for me," he said. "A quick catch-up with the family."

"Not easy, is it, fitting it all in. The wife left me at the beginning of the year, reckoned she couldn't take any more.

145

She should try being me." He grimaced. "Not a job for the faint-hearted, any of it." He fished in his inside jacket pocket, pulled out a notebook and flicked through the pages. "Stolen property, a lot of it, missing from containers found empty and abandoned."

"Would that be bags and watches?"

Dawlish nodded. "I'm investigating the theft of the bags and the murder of the lorry driver. The shipment he was carrying is worth a fortune to the retail market."

"Murder, you said."

"Cold blooded — a bullet to the back of the head, no messing around. The poor sod was left in the container to rot while they made off with the goods. When I read the report about the watches on the system, I spoke to your DCI. The bags were only stolen four days ago, so the trail is still hot," Dawlish said.

"I can add a little to what you have. So far, only two watches but several handbags have turned up in Leesdon. One of the watches was found on the wrist of a dead lad, the other was in the possession of a suspect. As for the bags, we found them in the lock-up of a dead market trader, who appears to have dealt in anything he could get his hands on. We believe that whoever is responsible for the robberies you're interested in has also stolen a number of pairs of expensive trainers."

"There'll be more. What we know about will just be the tip of the iceberg. This is robbery on a large scale and highly organised. They're interested only in the expensive end of things, like you say, designer goods. It's what happens to them once the thieves get their hands on them that intrigues me. The bags have serial numbers, like your watches and possibly the trainers, but so far none of them have turned up."

"They're stolen, then disappear. That doesn't make sense," Calladine said.

"We're not sure what's going on but it's a mystery I very much want an answer to."

"There've been two killings on my patch," Calladine told him. "One may not be directly related," he was thinking of

Noah Crosby, "but the other most certainly is. This market trader I mentioned was selling the trainers on his stall, and was found brutally beaten before being shot in the head. To date we have no idea who the killer is."

"Like our victim. Any chance of comparing bullets?" Dawlish said.

"How do I contact you?"

"If you're okay with it, I wouldn't mind hanging around for a couple of days. I intend to take a room at the hotel on the High Street."

Calladine had no problem with that. He handed Dawlish a card. "My details are on there. How do I contact you?"

Jeff Dawlish gave Calladine one of his in return. "First thing Monday then, Leesdon nick. D'you mind if I base myself at the station?"

"Not at all, you have Greco on board and I'm sure we can find you a desk. We can swap notes, map out similarities and I'll introduce you to the team."

"I brought the bullet that killed the lorry driver with me. Greco had it sent to your forensic people."

Calladine smiled. "Fine. We should have the results Monday afternoon."

Dawlish got to his feet. "Right then, I'd better go and sort myself a room."

Finishing up his tea, Calladine watched him walk away. Dawlish seemed okay. What he could add to the case, though, was anyone's guess.

CHAPTER THIRTY-TWO

Sunday

Calladine had hoped for a quiet Sunday. He'd like to have spent it catching up with home stuff and perhaps taking Kitty out for lunch. They could do with a talk, put things right, but the trill of his mobile at seven thirty in the morning put paid to all that.

It was Rocco. "We've got a body, sir. It looks like Luke Barton to me — beaten, shot in the back of the head and left to rot in the same alley we found Noah Crosby in."

Heaving a sigh, Calladine hauled himself out of bed. "Ruth know?"

"I'm ringing her next."

"I'll meet you at the crime scene. Give me half an hour." He stood up and straightened the empty bed. Kitty had chosen to stay at her own place last night. She'd rung him late on Saturday evening to tell him. Shame he had to work today of all days. The relationship badly needed attention he couldn't give it.

Within fifteen minutes, he'd showered and dressed. Sam, his dog, was whining. "You need a walk." With no Kitty he'd have to see to that himself but he didn't have the time. A quick glance out of the front window and he could see that his neighbours across the road were up and about. Ryan, the lad, was fond of Sam and often looked after him. "Want to go walkies with Ryan, old boy?" he said, and patted him. "Come on then, let's go and see if he's game."

* * *

Rocco had the area taped off and Natasha, Julian and their people were already in attendance.

Ruth sidled up beside Calladine. "I was hoping today would be a quiet one."

"Me too. I'd earmarked it for damage limitation, but no chance now."

"Kitty? What did I tell you. Carry on flirting with Amy like you have been and there was bound to be trouble."

"I don't flirt. Amy is an old friend. I expected Kitty to understand that."

"Your failing is not recognising when you're well off. Kitty is a good woman, you could have a future together if only you'd stop pissing her about."

Calladine was about to reply when they were interrupted by Julian. "The killing did not take place here," he said. "Once Natasha has the body back in the morgue I'll be able to tell you more."

"It looks very similar to the way Rob Knowles was killed," Natasha said, joining them. "I have both of them on my list for tomorrow. Knowles will be first, followed by Barton. With luck I'll find the bullets still lodged in their brains. Then I'll be able to tell you if the same gun was used on both."

"We have a DI from the Midlands on our patch," Calladine told them. "He is investigating a killing with a similar MO linked to the theft of the designer bags. Greco wants us to liaise with him. He has sent in a bullet for your team to examine," he told Julian.

"No problem," he said.

Calladine looked around. A crowd had gathered behind the tape and were no doubt speculating about what had happened. "Anyone hear or see anything?" he asked Rocco.

"If they did, they're not telling us. But people are scared, that I do know. There's a tension about the place that I don't much like."

Calladine inhaled and stuck his hands in his trouser pockets. Someone here knew something, he was sure. "Ask around, see what you can find out," he told Rocco. He turned to Ruth. "You and me had better go and speak to Barton's mother."

She groaned. "The job doesn't get any easier. This DI, has he got anything helpful to throw into the mix?"

"We only spoke briefly, we'll swap notes properly tomorrow," Calladine said.

"I spoke to Alice, she told me about the robberies that concern us, the bags and watches, but no mention of the trainers. That theft is more local, I feel," Ruth said.

He nodded. "I tend to agree. Knowles had loads of them. As for the other stuff we know about, Dawlish has the details. Regarding the trainers, favourite is Barton helping himself. As to how, we'd need to know a lot more about how that store operates."

"Well, Riley is unlikely to help," Ruth said. "He won't admit that anything is missing, remember."

Calladine smiled. "But we don't believe that for a moment, do we?" What they had to do now was find out more about the who and the when. That could well give them the lead that would identify the killers. "Barton's mother doesn't live far away. We'll take our own cars and then you can get off home when we're done."

"And you?" she asked.

"I don't have a family waiting."

Calladine climbed into his car and started the engine. He wasn't looking forward to telling Irene Barton about her son. She thought the police had arrested him. That was wrong, but she was bound to blame them, nevertheless.

CHAPTER THIRTY-THREE

Irene Barton was upset at the news of her son's murder. She was also livid. One minute she was in tears and the next she launched herself at Calladine, fists flying. She blamed him. Said he'd hounded her son, drawn attention to him from the wrong circles.

"What d'you mean by that?" he asked.

"My Luke was no saint but he wasn't really a wrong 'un. Lately he got in with a bad crowd, went along with stuff he should have avoided."

"Wrong circles, bad crowd? What're you talking about? Who was he involved with?" Calladine asked.

"You, questioning him. Next thing he's got that Spooner on his back. Spooner, or Spook as he's known, believes that my Luke has crossed him. He rang him several times, making threats. They even came to blows. It wasn't that long ago the pair of them were fighting in the street. Luke wouldn't say, but I'll lay odds it was Spooner who had him knifed a few days back."

Calladine knew the two didn't get on, but they'd questioned Spooner already and he had an alibi. "D'you have any proof of that?"

"Course not, Spooner's too clever for that," she scoffed. "I don't know the details but my Luke got into a spot of bother, he needed a helping hand but that Spooner went telling tales to the wrong people. When Luke found out, it didn't go down well, he was genuinely scared." A grim smile crossed her face. "He told me he intended to go away, disappear for a while. Said if he wanted to live, he had no choice. Then you lot came to the house and arrested him."

"Whoever took your son away, Mrs Barton, it wasn't us," Calladine assured her.

"Are you sure he didn't tell you what he was involved in or mention any names?" Ruth asked.

"No. Luke always said that if things got tricky it was better I didn't know anything. I quizzed him about it, course I did. I wanted to know if it had anything to do with Spooner, but he wouldn't say."

"Are you sure he didn't tell you anything else?" Calladine said.

She glared at him. "Look, you've just told me my son is dead. So forgive me if I'm not thinking straight, if I'm not up to the third degree from you lot." Irene Barton was shaking, she flopped down onto a chair and began to weep again. "I don't want to say anything that will blacken his name. He was young, easily influenced. He wasn't bad, deep down he wanted to live an honest life. He had that job at the garden centre and was doing well."

"We're not here to pin anything on your son, Mrs Barton," Calladine said gently. "And certainly not without evidence, but if we're to find who killed him, we need all the help we can get."

"Luke was selling stuff, to market traders mostly. I know he was no angel so I did suspect that it was probably knock-off. He was careful, said the one person he didn't want to find out was Spooner. God knows what he'd got himself into."

"D'you know what he was selling?" Calladine asked.

"No idea, but once I learned that Spooner was on his back I knew it was bound to be iffy. I never liked that lad even when he was small. He might come from money but he's always been dodgy. When you lot arrested Luke the other night, I thought Spook had dobbed him in."

"We didn't arrest your son," Ruth said. "Whoever took him, it wasn't the police."

"It would help if you could describe the men who came for him," Calladine said.

"Two big blokes, and one of them had a right mouth on him. To be honest, I did wonder at the time if they were genuine."

"Did they show you any identification?"

"One of them flashed something in front of my face but so quick I didn't have time to read it properly."

"When they took Luke, did they say how long he'd be gone?"

Irene Barton burst into tears again. "I should have stopped them. But they took me by surprise, and Luke didn't argue, he just went along with them."

"Mrs Barton, would you mind if we had a look at Luke's room?" Ruth asked.

"Why? What're you looking for?"

"Anything that points to who took your son," she said.

"Up the stairs, first on the left."

Ruth beckoned to Calladine and he followed her up the stairs. "I'd like to know more about what Barton was up to. If the trainers scam was down to him, who else was involved and where did he get them from?"

Calladine pulled open the drawers on the bedside cabinet and rummaged inside them. "Frequent phone calls, his mum said. Ah." He held up a mobile.

"A burner perhaps?"

Calladine examined it and nodded. "Pay as you go with a small balance and used to ring only one number. I'll get Julian's mob to take a look." Next, he moved onto the wardrobe but found nothing out of the ordinary.

Ruth was on her hands and knees looking under the bed. She pulled out a pair of shoes and then a long thin leather gun case. "Bingo! Looks like Barton was our shooter."

Calladine took the case from her, laid it on the bed and unzipped it. It was a rifle right enough, but was it the one used to shoot at Kitty's window?

"Spooner next?" Ruth asked.

"It's Sunday, will Jake be okay with that?"

"Let's speak to Spooner and then I'm off home." She smiled. "My absence will give him time to get the lunch on."

CHAPTER THIRTY-FOUR

Ricky Spooner wasn't home and his mother had no idea where he'd gone. "I'm not his keeper, he's twenty-four years old. He has the annex attached to the house and does as he pleases."

"When did you see him last?" Ruth asked. "This morning?"

"No, he wasn't at breakfast."

"Think carefully, Mrs Spooner, this is important. We need to find Ricky, he may be in danger." Calladine meant what he said, he wasn't trying to frighten her. So far they had three deaths, and although Barton's mother had given them her version of Ricky Spooner, they needed to find out the truth for themselves.

"Nonsense," she exclaimed. "My Ricky knows how to look after himself."

"D'you have his mobile number?" Calladine asked.

The woman handed him a card. "All his details are on there, but there won't be a problem. He's more than likely arranged to meet someone at the showroom."

"On a Sunday?" Ruth asked.

"We're open seven days a week and Ricky has to do his share."

Calladine was only half listening. He was on his own mobile, already calling Ricky. A look of relief crossed his face when he got an answer. "Mr Spooner, where are you? It's important we speak to you today."

"I'm out, a bit of business," Spooner said.

"I want you at the station within the hour. Fail to show and I'll put out a general call for you."

Calladine finished the call and beckoned for Ruth to follow him. "If I consider it necessary, I'll send him home in a patrol car and a uniformed officer will stay with you," he told Spooner's mother.

"A lot of fuss about nothing. My Ricky in danger, that's a ludicrous idea."

Out in the driveway, Ruth shook her head. "These mothers with sons who can do no wrong. D'you think Spooner killed Barton and the others?"

"My gut says no. In fact I think that if he's involved at all it's only on the periphery of the case. I'm guessing that any clout he has on the Hobfield was got by gossip and rumour. My worry is that now he's attracted the attention of someone bigger and more dangerous."

"Like who?"

"The blokes who took Barton away and probably murdered him. Spooner rubs them up the wrong way and he won't be so cocky," he said.

"Noah, Knowles, and now Barton. What have we uncovered, Tom?"

"I'm still trying to work that out myself. Noah and Barton had the mark incised onto their skin but Knowles didn't," Calladine said.

"Different killers? Are we looking at two different cases here?"

"Again my gut says no, but the evidence does suggest it. Noah doesn't fit the pattern but he was involved with the trainers scam, as was Knowles and Barton. Even Spooner was found on the Hobfield with a sports bag full of them. All have that in common." He looked at Ruth. "You should call it day now, get home to your family. I'll go back to the station and hang around for Spooner."

"You don't need me for the interview?"

"It'll be informal, more of a chat. I want to gain his trust, get his take on what's gone on," he said.

"Mrs Barton seemed sure enough that Spook is a bad 'un," Ruth said.

"We only have her word for it," Calladine said, "and we'd just told her that Luke was dead. Luke and Spook were enemies, he'd have fed his mother all sorts of lies to suit his own ends. Used Spooner as a way of getting her off his back."

"Or he's behind all this and a killer," Ruth parried.

Calladine shook his head. "As I said, I think Spooner has played a small part. He likely knows more than he's told us but I doubt he's got the guts for murder."

"Okay, if you're sure but go careful. I still don't trust him, far too slippery. I'll see you tomorrow. We've got the morgue first thing, don't forget."

Calladine pulled a face. Just what Monday mornings needed.

CHAPTER THIRTY-FIVE

When Calladine entered the main office he was surprised to see Alice still hard at work. "It is Sunday, you know. Don't you have a home to go to?"

"I wanted another look through the file, sir." She smiled. "Anyway, just as well someone's here. We've had a call from Mrs Seddon, her son Killian hasn't turned up yet. He's been missing since Friday night and she's frantic with worry. She asked if you'd call round."

Calladine nodded. He'd call in on his way home, but what reassurance he could offer was difficult to say. He hoped not but for all they knew Killian could be lying dead somewhere, having fallen foul of the men who'd killed the others.

"Also IT forensics have cleaned up that photo of whoever drove Noah to the Hobfield after that last robbery. We got a partial registration number and I ran it through the computer. There are four possibles within the Leesworth area, and one of them belongs to Goddard's Garden Centre," she said.

"A transit type? Navy blue?"

"That's the one."

Barton had worked for Goddard's so it made sense. He'd check with them later, ask if he had use of the van in his own time. "Good work. Anything else?"

"No, sir. I'm ploughing through everything we've got but I'm no nearer to formulating a theory about the killer."

"You and me both, Alice," he said, going into his office. At least they could rule out Barton. His part in this appeared to have been the person selling the trainers locally, like Noah. But where they got them from was still a mystery. Rumour had it that Noah worked for Barton. If the van proved to be the one they were looking for, that would appear to be true. Perhaps Barton cut Noah in on the deal, let the lad make some money selling a few pairs. All very well in theory, but there were still too many possibles for Calladine's liking.

Jeff Dawlish had left a file on his desk. Calladine sat down and began to trawl through it. It featured a number of robberies from long distance lorries carrying expensive goods — the bags and the watches to name only two. Interestingly, the goods were all heading north and appeared to have been targeted at two particular service stations. These stations were large and offered facilities for drivers to take showers, have a rest and get a meal. Where the drivers hadn't been around, the load had been stolen, but on the two occasions the drivers had remained in their cabs and had tried to stop the thieves, they'd ended up brutally beaten and shot through the head.

Alice stuck her head round his door. "Ricky Spooner is waiting for you downstairs, sir."

He nodded. Time to get serious. Whether he liked it or not, Spooner must be made to appreciate the danger he could be in.

* * *

The young man was seated at a table in one of the interview rooms. Calladine joined him, deliberately leaving the door open. "I'm pleased you came in for a chat, Ricky. I need to speak to you."

"Always happy to help."

"I'm a little concerned about some information that's come my way. Rumour has it that you're involved in the sale of stolen high-end trainers."

Spooner shook his head, tutting. "Rumour, Mr Calladine. First watches and now the trainers have reared their ugly head again. If I were you I wouldn't take any notice. Someone is making mischief."

Calladine smiled. "Ordinarily I would dismiss it, but everyone else who's been involved in selling the trainers has been murdered." He paused for a few seconds. "So you see my problem. Your name has come up, and I have a duty to protect you."

"Surely, you should be chasing the killer, not wasting time sitting here chatting to me," Spooner said.

"Oh, I am and we're close. But until I've got those responsible under lock and key, I dare not take any risks." Calladine watched Spooner. He appeared calm enough. "I know you had several pairs of these trainers. You were stopped and searched on the Hobfield. The incident is logged and the number of shoes you had on you is in the report. Ten pairs, Ricky, and different sizes, so not for personal use, I think."

"Trainers, you say. Come to think of it I was offered a pair. That young Crosby lad had some for sale as I recall."

"That night you were carrying more than one pair."

Spooner heaved a sigh and asked. "Do I need a solicitor?"

CHAPTER THIRTY SIX

"That's your choice but I don't intend to take you to task for anything, not yet anyway. What I need, Ricky, is information. I'm after cold blooded killers. A few pairs of trainers are not the main feature here."

"You want me to snitch, become a grass?"

Calladine shrugged. He was surprised, surely that tag didn't bother Spooner. "If that's what it takes. People have been murdered. Rob Knowles, the market trader, and Luke Barton who worked at Goddard's, as well as young Noah. Currently Killian Seddon is missing and no one's seen him in over twenty-four hours. I don't know what part, if any, he is playing in this, but the fact we can't find him is making me twitchy."

As the words sank in Spooner turned pale. The news had obviously shocked him. "They got Barton too? Was it, like, bad?"

"Yes. He was killed much like Knowles. Beaten to a pulp and finished off with a bullet to the back of the head. These people are not playing games, Ricky. They're hardcore and need taking off the streets."

Spooner looked decidedly sick. He was shaking. "I'd no idea it was this serious. I heard about poor Noah, the news about what happened to him got round in no time. I knew he was taking a risk. He was playing Barton and me off against each other. He kept up his friendship with both of us while using his connection with us to suit his own ends."

"What d'you mean?" Calladine asked.

"I suspect he told tales. Noah worked at the garden centre with Barton, he was a clever lad, he saw things and spoke about them. Barton wasn't as honest as he should have been, always on the take."

"What did Noah see?"

"Barton stealing stuff for a start. He had sticky hands, is what Noah used to say. Stock would come in and Barton would doctor the delivery notes and keep the odd item for himself."

Calladine wondered if any of these 'odd items' had been the trainers from Northern or the other stuff they were interested in.

"As for Knowles," Spooner continued, "why kill him in such a horrific way? He sold stuff on the market, he was no crook."

No, he wasn't, but he obviously didn't choose his business associates wisely. "I reckon Barton was offloading the stolen goods, the trainers for instance, on Knowles, getting him to sell them for a cut." Spooner nodded at this. "Will you help me, Ricky? Tell me everything you know."

Spooner looked down, no doubt thinking hard about his position. "It's grassing, and I'd be tainted with it forever. People around here don't forget."

"C'mon, that's not going to worry a man like you, you don't live on the Hobfield. Anyway, it's a small price to pay to stop the killings, perhaps even yours. You should see what was done to Knowles and Barton. Whoever the killer or killers are, they've got nothing to lose now."

"And you think I'm in danger?" Spooner looked up.

"You could be, Ricky. It all depends on how involved you are."

Spooner fell silent. He sat staring down at his hands. "I'm not involved, not really," he said finally. "I simply saw an opportunity to make some easy money and took it."

"Surely you're not short of money, not coming from a family like yours?"

His head shot up. "That's the trouble, Mr Calladine, they treat me like a kid, especially my mother. And then there's the 'work ethic'. God, how she bangs on about that one. Forever telling me how hard my dad worked to build the business and the long hours he had to put in."

"I remember your dad as it happens. He was a good man."

"Well I'm not him. I want the money but I'm not so keen on the work or the long hours." He shrugged. "All right, I'm a lazy bugger, nothing wrong with that."

"At least you're honest about it. So what happened, how d'you find out about the trainers?" Calladine asked.

"Noah Crosby, he had about a dozen pairs he wanted to offload. I knew they were expensive and the genuine article, but I also knew they weren't in the shops yet and that bothered me. I reckoned if I sold them about the town they'd attract the wrong attention."

"So what did you do with them, Ricky?" Calladine said.

"I gave them back to Noah. He wasn't bothered, said I was being soft and that there was a ready market for them." He laughed. "A sixteen-year-old kid telling me I'm soft. I stood there and took it too."

"Noah was wearing a pair when we found his body. D'you know where the lad got them from?"

"No idea, possibly wherever he got the other stuff from. The only items that interested me were the watches. He offered to sell me one cheap and I jumped at the chance. I should have questioned him but didn't. Saw a bargain and went for it." He smiled ruefully. "Noah said that the stock turnover was fast and that next week there'd be new stuff. He didn't say who he got the trainers and watches from, said the less I knew, the better."

"Did you ever go to a lock-up belonging to Rob Knowles?" Calladine asked.

Spooner shook his head. "No, I don't know the man. Is that where Noah got the trainers from?" He gave a shrug.

"I'm not daft, I did realise they had to be stolen but there was no hue and cry. No one appeared to be missing them, or the watches and bags either."

"You and Noah fell out, what was that all about?"

"He was an angry little sod, always at odds with someone on that estate about something. He was far too volatile. He'd taken to robbing shops too, did you know that? He targeted those that stayed open late where there'd be only one person working. The lad was relentless, a one person crime wave. I got sick and tired of it. I didn't want anything more to do with his little scams and told him so. It was a simple choice to end our relationship. But I knew Barton would soon get sick of him too. Sooner or later he was bound to discover that Noah was ripping him off and do something about it. Barton was an animal. It wouldn't surprise me if it was him that killed Noah."

"Are you aware of the rumours circulating on the estate about the turf war raging between you and Barton?"

Spooner laughed. "I'm not given to waging war with anybody, Mr Calladine."

From what Spooner had told him, Calladine thought this was probably true. The young man had been candid in his answers and now it was getting late. Time to wind this up. "I'm going to have an officer keep watch on your home, just to be on the safe side. I'll want a statement setting down what we've spoken about today. Thanks for the info. I'm sure it'll help."

CHAPTER THIRTY-SEVEN

Spooner was taken home in a patrol car. It was time to call it a day. Calladine grabbed his jacket and went out into the main office.

"Alice, I must insist, go home, you've done enough for one day."

"Mrs Seddon rang in, sir. Killian has turned up but she still wants to see you."

A huge relief and a load off Calladine's mind, but the last thing he needed right now was a screaming match with the Seddons. "Ring her for me, would you? Apologise and tell her I'll pop in tomorrow."

Alice nodded. "Don't blame you, there's not a lot of the day left."

Calladine gave her a wave and made for the staircase. He was mulling over what Spooner had told him. Was the bad reputation undeserved, the so called turf war non-existent? If so, why were the kids on the estate so sure it was genuine? Had they simply taken Barton's word for it or was he missing something? Calladine was too tired to work it out. All he wanted now was a meal and to put his feet up. On his way out of the station, he rang Eve and told her he couldn't make dinner. He didn't want to let her down but he really couldn't face all that small talk with the other family members. She was disappointed but he'd make it up to her once the case was sorted.

When he reached his cottage he knew at once that his quiet night was wishful thinking. Ken Lovell had the sitting room stripped of wallpaper, his ladders erected and was busy painting the ceiling.

"The paper you chose, I'm picking it up tomorrow. Get this done and gloss the paintwork and I should have it finished in a couple of days. Kitty gave me a key, so no need to worry about letting me in," he said.

Calladine looked round, there were sheets over his furniture and Sam had taken himself off to sit at the top of the stairs. Good of Kitty to tell him. He'd no idea this was happening today and given how he felt, could have done without it.

"Kitty?" he asked.

"Round at hers. She said to tell you to forget tonight, she's busy working and she'll see you tomorrow."

Great. No meal and no Kitty to take out for one. What was he supposed to do now? He felt decidedly uncomfortable in the company of this man. How did you make small talk with a man who'd lost his son in those circumstances? And what if Lovell asked about Alfie, how could he square the lack of progress? "Fancy a cuppa?" Calladine asked finally.

Tea was one thing but if Lovell was expecting an update on the hit and run investigation, Calladine would come unstuck. He had nothing to tell him and right now that was making him feel guilty, as if he hadn't tried hard enough. The unasked question hung in the air between them.

"I like mine strong, that do you?"

Lovell nodded and clambered down the ladder. "Nice little cottages these, solid, been here years."

This street and the people in it were something the detective could talk about. "I was born in one a few doors down. I've lived round here all my life."

"My dad remembers your mother and that gangster cousin of yours."

He was talking about Ray Fallon. "We can't choose our family," Calladine said. "I had no choice in the matter. My mum raised us both. Fortunately, we turned out complete opposites."

"You both went into crime though." His face expressionless, Lovell asked, "Any closer to finding who killed my lad?"

Here it was, and it turned Calladine's stomach. This was ridiculous, he'd have to tell him something. "We're looking at flecks of paint found on your — well, on Alfie's clothing."

"Red paint," Lovell said.

Calladine's head shot up. "Why d'you say that?"

"Must have been something I heard."

"I wouldn't listen to gossip, Ken, doesn't do any good as a rule. And it wasn't red as it happens. So don't go suspecting every driver of a red car you can recall from that time."

"It was a red car, the one found burnt out on the rough ground. I'm right, aren't I, have to be."

"I'm given to understand the car was badly burned and the forensic people couldn't get much from it."

"I did a job for a technician who works at the Duggan, and he said it were red." Ken Lovell swigged the remainder of his tea and got back to work. He didn't look happy — memories of his young son, no doubt. Calladine took the mugs into the kitchen, called to Sam, and slipped on his lead.

"I'm off to walk the dog," he said. "Lock up when you've done."

Calladine felt rattled, disappointed at the scant progress made in the boy's case. Lovell deserved better, but what was the betting they'd get no further with it?

CHAPTER THIRTY-EIGHT

Calladine took Sam across the road to Ryan's. The dog wagged his tail and licked the lad's hand. He was as pleased to be leaving Lovell to it as Calladine was.

"The decorator's in and Sam's not happy. I've got something to do, would you mind?"

With a grin, Ryan stood aside to let Sam in. "I'll take him for a run later, don't worry, he'll have a great time."

Calladine left them to it, not what he'd planned but there wasn't much he could do. Kitty had decided the place was getting a make-over and that was that. He wandered up Leesdon High Street. He had a lot on his mind, not least the case. The body count was growing but they were no further forward. Suddenly he heard a car horn and he turned round.

"You look lost. Something up?"

It was Ruth. Calladine felt a sudden rush of relief. "You're spot on — lost just about sums it up."

"Get in," she ordered. "You eaten?"

"I've been speaking to Spooner. I was hoping for a quiet evening but Kitty's put paid to that. She's got Lovell in decorating and he's asking tricky questions."

"You can't blame him for that. He wants answers and doesn't understand the complexity of the job. You can eat at ours. I've done a roast and there's way too much. Afterwards you can put your feet up and have forty winks. You look done in."

"Won't Jake mind?"

"No, and Harry will be thrilled. He'll see you as yet another toy to play with."

During the few minutes it took to get to Ruth's, Calladine gave her the salient points of his chat with Spooner.

"You think he's in the clear, don't you? In fact from your tone I'd say you actually like him." She shook her head. "I'm not so sure. Think smoke and fire, Tom. Those rumours didn't come from nowhere. I've spent time on the estate recently, mixing with the younger element. I've listened to the kids and they are genuinely afraid of him."

"We've nothing on him," Calladine said.

"The watch and the trainers, isn't that a start?"

"He explained about those."

Ruth gave him doubtful look. "Tells you he didn't do it and you believe him. What's happened to you, Calladine? You've gone all soft. Siding with the villains isn't usually your thing."

They pulled up in Ruth's drive. She took a bag of shopping from the boot and the pair went inside. "Jake's in the garden, he's trying to teach Harry to kick a ball." She plonked the shopping bag on the kitchen table and checked the oven.

The smell was glorious. "Roast beef?" he asked.

"Yes, so you can't say I don't spoil you."

Calladine went outside to join Jake and Harry. "She's invited me to dinner," he explained to Jake.

He smiled and nodded at the small goal net he'd erected on the far side of the lawn. "I'll be goalkeeper and you and Harry can try and get one past me."

Harry giggled and in a flurry of little legs, ran towards the ball. Launching at it with his right foot, he sent the ball spinning towards his father.

"He's a natural," Jake said. "Keep this up and he'll be playing for Leesworth before long."

Ruth called out. "One of you can set the table, dinner's nearly ready."

"That'll be me then," Jake said. To Harry, he said, "Why don't you go inside and show Uncle Tom your train set?"

The little lad whooped with laughter and ran towards the back door.

"He's got it set up in the conservatory. Help yourself to a drink," Jake said.

Calladine saw the whisky bottle on the cabinet in the conservatory and had to admit he could down a generous glug. He hadn't so much as tasted the stuff since his illness, and given the way the day had gone, he felt he deserved one. But Ruth would pull a face and go on at length about his past bad habits. Giving in now would be letting her down and he could do without the guilt.

"I'm watching you, Calladine. Touch that bottle and you're on the naughty step all week."

He smiled. "Wasn't going to, honest."

Ruth gave him a doubtful look and wagged her finger at him and Harry. "Right, you pair. Hands washed and get yourselves to the table."

With some amusement, Calladine watched the little lad immediately do his mother's bidding. There was no doubt about it, Ruth had her menfolk well trained.

CHAPTER THIRTY NINE

Monday

Monday, Calladine had an early start. He had a lot on. He wanted to brief the team, arrange a meeting with Jeff Dawlish and then there was the morgue and the two post-mortems. He'd arrived home on Sunday night well fed, and feeling much better. Lovell had left for the day too, so there were no more tricky conversations. Kitty had rung to say she'd be busy all day with work and it could go on into the evening. He didn't argue with her, there was no point. But a good night's sleep and with everything slipping back into perspective, he felt more like his old self.

Sam had stayed over with Ryan, not that Calladine minded. The dog loved the lad and Ryan loved him back. They were good together and the lad could give Sam so much more than he could. Regular walks for a start. Ryan was happy to keep him for the rest of the day, so Lovell would have the place to himself.

Calladine drove the short distance to the station and parked up. Ruth had been a real friend yesterday, but after the meal she had again taken him to task over Spooner. She didn't believe that he was an innocent party in all this. She put forward a convincing argument too, but Calladine didn't need the case complicating by rumour and Ruth's gut instinct, he was more than capable of coming unstuck trusting his own. But he couldn't simply dismiss what she said either. For now, he decided to reserve judgement.

The team were already at their desks, Dawlish too. He'd taken possession of the spare at the back of the main office.

"Several things today," Calladine began. "Ruth and I have an appointment at the morgue. It's the post-mortems of Rob Knowles and Luke Barton this morning. I'm not expecting any surprises but you never know." He looked at Rocco. "You and Alice visit the Seddon family. Try to find out why Killian took off the way he did, ask if he's afraid of something, or someone. The Seddon lads have held back all through this case and now we need the truth. I'd like to know where those watches and handbags came from. How they slipped through the hands of the original thieves and ended up in a Leesdon lock-up. Once Ruth and I have finished at the Duggan Centre we'll have another word with Marcus Goddard. They have a van that I suspect was involved in the shop robberies and possibly the hit and run of young Alfie Lovell."

He looked at Dawlish. "Want to join us? Get a flavour for our investigation so far?"

"If it's okay with you, I thought I'd speak to the manager of the sportswear store, Riley. Something is very wrong there. I've checked and double checked and I can't find any record of there being a recent robbery of the type of trainers we're interested in."

Calladine nodded, a good call. He had a theory of his own that what happened with the trainers had to be local. "Right then, back here this afternoon for feedback." He paused and looked round at the array of serious faces. "I know how hard you're all working but you can't have failed to realise that the case is going nowhere. We need a break, something has to give and I'm relying on all of you."

Calladine had never been more serious. He had no idea who was behind the killings, and given that the murder of Noah

Crosby was different from the others, they had to come to terms with the possibility of there being at least two killers at large.

* * *

"This one is really winding you up, isn't it?"

Calladine nodded, Ruth was right on that score. "I've never wanted a breakthrough more, and I can't get it out of my head that I've missed something. There's something niggling me, something at the back of my mind but I can't think what it is."

"The case is complex and all we've got so far are bodies. Try relaxation techniques, to clear your mind, or even meditation, Amy should be able to help you with that one. And don't pull that face, it's worth a try if whatever is niggling you suddenly pops back into your mind."

"I am not consulting a fortune teller about my case. For goodness sake, what sort of detective would that make me?"

"A human one, one who isn't scared to use all the resources available to him. And you're forgetting that Amy has helped us before."

"I must have been mad."

"It can't do any harm and no one needs to know. It can be our little secret." She giggled.

"See, you don't mean a word of it. You're just trying to embarrass me, Bayliss."

"I would never do that. I'm on your side and so is Amy. The problem with this case is all the facts and personalities involved in it. Then there is the old 'Shadow' case. Where does that fit in, if at all?"

"I'm hoping it has nothing to do with what we're about now."

"Interesting though, it means that someone out there knows as much as you do about the old case and the details that were never released to the press. Ask yourself, where did he get them?"

Calladine hadn't given it much thought, too busy with the murders. But perhaps he should. Was it possible that it had a bearing on their current investigation?

CHAPTER FORTY

It was going to be a long morning at the morgue and not a pleasant one.

True to form, Dr Natasha Barrington had everything prepared, including the bodies of Rob Knowles and Luke Barton.

"I've had a preliminary look at both," she said. "And done all the necessary X-rays. In my opinion, the injuries sustained prior to the gunshot to the head were similar. In fact, I suspect the same weapon was used to beat them with. Some sort of metal bar, or pipe."

Ruth squirmed. "Not a good way to go."

"We'll do Knowles first," Natasha continued. "He was the first of the two to be found."

Calladine and Ruth stood on the viewing platform above where Natasha and her team were working.

"Let's hope there are no surprises," Calladine whispered.

Ruth nodded. "You're thinking the incised marks on the skin."

Natasha heard her and looked up. "There aren't, not on Knowles anyway, I've already checked. Barton has one on his arm, but you already know about that."

"That just makes things more complicated. Some have the marks, some don't. It doesn't make sense," Ruth said.

Natasha began. "Knowles was found taped to a chair, his hands and his ankles bound together. He was also gagged, so he was unable to say anything or move. He has extensive damage to both hands. The X-rays show that the finger bones and joints in both hands are smashed. The ulna and radius bones in both forearms are broken, as are the bones in both lower legs."

"He took some beating," Ruth whispered. "Despite being gagged he must have tried to scream, whimper or something. I can't believe that no one heard anything."

"He was found in that empty flat on the ground floor of Heron House. A young mother with her infant and an elderly couple are the only other occupants on that floor. The young mother isn't for talking and the elderly couple heard nothing. Whoever did this chose their location well," Calladine said.

"Local knowledge?" Ruth averted her eyes — Natasha was fishing around in Knowles's brain.

"I've got the bullet." She held it up. "Now we'll do Barton."

Luke Barton had injuries to his limbs very similar to those found on Knowles.

"Do you know where this one was killed?"

"Not yet," Calladine said.

"It would help to know," Natasha said. "There's most likely forensic evidence. Looking at the marks on his body the injuries could have been made with the same weapon. We've taken swabs and blood samples already, Julian might come up with something." She nodded to her technician. "Let's see if we can find the bullet that killed this one."

Moments later the bullet was out and in a labelled bag next to the one that killed Knowles. Ballistics would find out if they came from the same gun.

"I'll let you have my report by tomorrow morning," she promised. "And no doubt Julian will be in touch. But initially I can tell you that both men suffered the same fate, the beating and finally the bullet to the head. Knowles, as you know, was in an empty flat in Heron House but Barton was

175

dumped. Find where he was killed and Julian may be able to tell you more."

"Coffee?" Ruth asked.

"A large whisky would be more appropriate," Calladine said.

"Not for you it wouldn't. We're health conscious these days, remember."

Calladine nodded. How could he forget? Certainly not while he had Ruth on his tail.

"I am confused though," she said on the way out. "Why the X-mark on Noah and on Barton when he got injured, but not on Knowles and not when Barton was killed? It doesn't make sense."

"It does if we're looking at two different cases."

Ruth pulled a face. "Please don't say that. We've got enough on with the trainers thing. You can't seriously believe that the incised marks are something to do with this 'shadow' from the past?"

"No, I don't, but I think it might have something to do with someone who recalls the case or has been told about it since."

"Now you're being cryptic and it doesn't suit you."

"Goddard's next," he merely said. "We need to find that blue transit type van, then we need to have another look at Knowles's lock-up, see if anything left intact might have come from Goddard's."

"But the garden centre first. They have a café and do a nice breakfast, fancy some?" Ruth said.

He smiled. "Bacon barm?"

"Not for you. Wholemeal toast and coffee or forget it. I don't want Kitty on my back for leading you astray."

"Life's no fun anymore and I'm fast getting fed up. All this health stuff, it's not doing my thought processes much good, you know. I still can't pinpoint what is niggling at me and it's doing my head in."

"We could go to Goddard's via Julian's apartment and see Amy. She'd put you right."

Calladine knew Ruth didn't realise how important this 'niggle' was, she treated it like a joke. But he knew different. There was something he'd been told or seen and it hadn't registered at the time. The answer to this case was in his head but he was damned if he could remember what it was.

CHAPTER FORTY-ONE

"We'll compromise," Ruth said as they left the Duggan. "We'll ditch breakfast at Goddard's and have coffee at Amy's later."

"All right," Calladine said. "But start going on about meditation and all that stuff and I'll leave the pair of you to it."

Ruth, who was driving, came off the bypass and turned into the road that would take them to the garden centre. "When we park up I'll give her a ring, tell her we're coming. I'm due a catch-up with Amy anyway. A quick coffee will do no harm."

Goddard's was as busy as ever. Ruth headed for the office to find Marcus, calling Amy as she went. Calladine wandered off towards the centre's parked up vehicles. All sported the 'Goddards' name and logo on the side except one, a dark blue, transit type, well scratched and with a sizeable dent in the bumper. Bending down for a closer look at the scratches, he could see that at one time the van had been white but had had a respray.

Ruth was approaching with Marcus in tow. "This van, Mr Goddard, who uses it?" Calladine asked.

"No one now, it was the one Barton drove when he was delivering. I daren't trust him with anything else, he wasn't the most careful driver in the world and our others are expensive to fix or replace."

"You've probably heard that Barton's been found dead."

He nodded. "Got the culprit yet?"

Ignoring this, Calladine asked, "Who else used this van apart from Barton?"

"No one, and I let him use it in his own time too."

"I want our forensic people to take a look. I'd appreciate you keeping it locked and not letting anyone touch it. I'll send someone to pick it up within the hour."

Marcus Goddard didn't appear put out by this. "Take it away by all means, the keys are in the ignition. In fact, you can keep it for me. Is that all?"

Not the reaction Calladine had expected. So far Marcus was on the periphery of the case but he was beginning to wonder if the young man was involved. The van had showed up any number of times — the shot at Kitty's window being one of the most significant. But if he was, why was Marcus so casual about them taking it?

The pair watched him stroll off back toward the shop. He gave the impression of not having a care in the world.

Ruth tapped Calladine's head. "What's going on in there?"

"Is he involved? What d'you think?"

"We've no reason to think so. He's always very cool about it all. If this van is implicated in anything, I reckon he's been kept in the dark," Ruth said.

But Calladine wasn't so sure. "Nothing and no one is as they appear in this case, Ruth, and I'm thoroughly sick of it."

"Amy's next," she said. "We'll have that cuppa and you can have a quick chat."

He sighed. "You do realise that Amy knows nothing about this case, so I don't know what makes you think she can help us."

"We'll see," said Ruth enigmatically. "You just never know."

* * *

Fortunately for Amy, Julian's apartment was a decent size, so she had room to spread out. "He's been very good about all my clutter," she said. "He never complains, but the sooner I find something of my own the better. Julian is a proper sweetie but he does like his solitude and he's got an odd taste in music."

Then Amy shook her head. "You're troubled, Tom. It's oozing from every pore." She gestured towards a small table and two chairs. "Come and sit down here with me."

"Look, this is silly," he muttered. "It won't achieve anything."

"You never know. You might be in for a surprise. What's wrong? Tell me about the problem."

Neither of them was going to give up. Calladine gave another deep sigh and decided to go with it. "It's the case we're working on. I've read every word in the case files, listened to hours of chat from various folk we've interviewed. In among it all something was said that's important, might even be crucial, but I can't for the life of me recall what it was."

She nodded. "A chance remark that went unnoticed."

"Yes."

Amy handed him a pack of cards. "Shuffle them, and while you do, think about the case."

"They're those weird cards, the ones you use in your readings."

"Yes, and they might be able to help you." While Calladine shuffled, Amy glanced at Ruth and smiled. "Now hand them back to me. Don't worry, I'm not going to make this complicated, just a simple overview will do for now." Amy placed three cards face down on the table and turned the first one over. She smiled at Calladine. "The Hermit. He represents you, the seeker in the darkness, looking for light."

"A bit fanciful."

"Nonetheless true," she said, and turned over the second card. "The Seven of Swords. In this context, I take the card to represent a thief who operates in secret. He's an accomplished liar and will turn events to his own advantage." She met Calladine's gaze. "This is a man, young, and not what he seems. He may have already taken you in, pulled the wool over your eyes about his true nature."

He shrugged. "That could refer to any number of young men connected with this case. Most of them in fact. Anything else?"

Amy turned over the final card, the Two of Swords. "As you might say yourself, Tom, this man is a right piece of work. An expert at fooling people and getting his own way. A man skilled in duplicity who right now is taking great delight in fooling you." Amy closed her eyes. "But he has slipped up. You are right in thinking as much. He said something the last time you spoke, which is what didn't register in your mind. It's important. He made a mistake and gave himself away, so this is your chance."

Ruth went over to join them. "Are you saying that this man is someone Tom doesn't suspect but should?"

Amy nodded. "A young man who gives a convincing account of himself but it is all lies." She gave the remaining cards a shuffle. "Choose one final card."

Calladine took one and handed it to her.

His choice made her frown. "The Eight of Swords. Given the others, this card signifies incarceration." She looked at him. "Someone serving a prison sentence and if not the driving force behind what is going on, they are very close to the perpetrator."

CHAPTER FORTY-TWO

Rocco and Alice pulled up outside the Seddon house on the Hobfield. Rocco had already spoken to Killian and reckoned the running away incident was attention seeking. "Realistically, what can he tell us that we don't already know?"

"You never know with kids, Rocco. He and his brother mix with everyone on the Hobfield. Let's keep an open mind," Alice said.

Rocco still wasn't convinced. "I've gone through the case file umpteen times and he's not really involved. Granted he knew Noah Crosby, but so did most people on the estate."

Rocco knocked on the door and the pair waited. After several more raps, Mrs Seddon opened it and let them in. "He knows it's you and he's run up to his room, locked the door and won't come out. I haven't a clue what's got into him. He's been a nervous wreck for two days now."

"Did something happen to scare him?" Alice asked.

The woman shrugged. "It was on the local radio about Barton. After he heard the report he went to his room. I went up with his supper Friday night and he'd scarpered. He stayed out overnight, all day Saturday and came back Sunday morning. He's said nowt, not even where he's been, only that he doesn't want to see or talk to anyone. I told him I was calling you lot, but it's made no difference."

"Can I go up, knock on his bedroom door?" Rocco asked.

"If you want but I doubt you'll get much. Whatever's up has changed him, made Killian afeared of his own shadow."

"Does your Dean know what this is about?" Alice asked watching Rocco make for the staircase.

"They talk about some stuff, but not this. I've asked our Dean but he's as puzzled as I am."

The two women fell silent, listening to Rocco knock on Killian's bedroom door.

"Want to talk?" Rocco called to him. "If there's anything bothering you, perhaps I can help."

"Go away, no one can help. I'm not coming out and I'm not talking to anyone."

Rocco tried the door, it was locked like his mum had said. He could stand here all day and get nowhere. "Look, I'll slip my card under your door. Change your mind and I'll come round again. Just give me a ring."

Badgering him was pointless. Perhaps when he'd had time to think things through he'd be more amenable.

Rocco returned downstairs to the others. "You've got our numbers. Anything changes, just let us know. But there's not a lot we can do if Killian won't speak to us."

"The lad's an idiot. He's suffering, I know he is, but I haven't got a clue what it's about." She looked at the pair. "These murders — Barton and Knowles — you get anyone for them?"

"Not yet, Mrs Seddon, but we're close," Rocco lied.

"I worry that he's got himself mixed up in something he can't get out of. This estate is poison for boys his age. Ask my Dean, he's had his fair share of it."

"Where is Dean?" Alice asked.

"He's got himself a part-time job at the newsagents. He'll be back later."

They went back to the car.

"What d'you think?" Alice asked

"He's either in this up to his neck or it's attention seeking."

"He ran away and now he's locked himself in his room. Whatever the reason, Rocco, as far as Killian is concerned it's deadly serious."

"We've enough to do without mollycoddling teenage lads," he said.

* * *

Jeff Dawlish parked in front of the Northern Sportswear store and sat for several minutes, watching the to and fro of customers. The place was busy, lots of footfall but there was nothing in the window about the impending launch of the new trainers.

The bags and watches were stolen and had disappeared but not the trainers, it seemed. Dawlish was intrigued and wanted to know more. Time to introduce himself.

"Mr Riley, I'm DI Dawlish, Midlands Serious Crime Squad. Can I have a word?"

Riley turned pale. He backed away, looking terrified. "Look, I told the other detective everything I know. There's nothing I can add."

"I know you did, but I like to poke around myself, get a proper feel for a case." Dawlish looked around the store. "They're not on sale yet, I see. When is the launch?"

"You mean the trainers," Riley whispered. "Two days' time."

"Would you mind if I had a look at your stock?"

"Actually, I would. The trainers are under lock and key. They're quite safe, Mr Dawlish. If you've any doubts ask your colleague, DI Calladine, he's already been here and looked over the stock."

Dawlish shook his head. "The trainers have been clan-destinely on sale in this area for a while. I think you have to agree that something is wrong. I'm now part of the team trying to find out what that is. So if you don't mind, I'd like to take a look for myself."

"No," Riley said firmly. "You want to come nosing around here, get a warrant."

"If that's how you want it. But you can't keep this up much longer. You're stock down and sooner or later that will become evident."

Dawlish left Riley to it and returned to his car. He rang Calladine and told him his suspicions. "Riley knows more than he's told us and he's terrified. I would appreciate a closer look at that stock of his, rule the trainers in or out of the thieving I'm investigating. Problem is, he's insisting I get a warrant."

"If that's his game, I'll get it organised," Calladine said.

CHAPTER FORTY-THREE

"Trouble?" Ruth asked.

"Dawlish wants a closer look at Riley's stock and I can't say I blame him," Calladine said. "We know that the bags and watches were stolen as part of a much bigger operation but not the trainers. Alice has done extensive research and found nothing."

"What're you saying?"

"That the trainers are a local crime. Someone — my current thinking is Barton — got wind of the expected delivery to Riley's store and helped themselves to a few dozen pairs."

"An interesting theory, but how do we prove it?" she said.

"I'm not sure but my money's on Barton. He had a part time job there until a fortnight ago."

"Riley told us that Barton worked there for no more than a few days. He didn't like him, remember. So if he did steal the trainers he'd have had to have worked pretty damn quick. What does Dawlish expect to find?" she asked.

"Missing trainers, boxes with nothing in them, something like that."

"If the trainers are down to local thieving, doesn't that just complicate things?" Ruth asked. "How do they fit in with the other stuff, the bags and watches?"

"I suspect a relatively small number were stolen by Barton."

Ruth was still puzzled. "We know where Barton got the trainers from and what he did with them. He supplied market traders like Knowles, but what about the other stuff, the watches and handbags, where did they come from?"

"That bit has been bothering me too," Calladine admitted. "There's not the volume around to be the entire load that was stolen. Barton again? He saw his chance with the trainers, did he find out where the other goods were being held?"

"And helped himself to some of it. It's possible and if you're right then it'd probably be local," Ruth said.

"We'll have another scout around Knowles's lock-up before we return to the station," Calladine said. "Make sure we've not missed anything. You drive while I get that warrant sorted for Dawlish."

They were sitting in the car park at the back of Leesdon Library going over everything but what Amy had just said to him. Ruth nudged him. "Well, c'mon. You've said nowt. What did you think about your meeting with Amy?"

Calladine pulled a face. "I'm not sure, but she could be right about one thing and if she is we've got a bigger problem than I thought."

"What thing? What problem?"

"The incarcerated man she spoke about. I'm thinking Mark Goddard."

CHAPTER FORTY-FOUR

Ruth stared at him. "You can't seriously think that Mark Goddard is behind what's been going on?"

"Why not? You meet some useful people inside."

"But you said it was Lena who was the planner, and that Mark didn't have that much about him."

"He was still a violent criminal and happy to take risks," Calladine said. "Lena was his steadying influence. She might be running this latest scam with him for all we know."

"Mark Goddard is inside, d'you really believe that there wouldn't have been a whisper by now? He might meet some useful people there but he'll meet some double-crossing individuals too. I'm talking about the ones only too happy to stick the knife in."

She was right as always, but Amy's words had got him thinking. "The one thing Mark did have was contacts. He went down for several high profile robberies. He would still be at it if someone hadn't got killed."

"There is nothing about the Goddard family's set-up to arouse suspicion. Lena doesn't like you, fair enough, but Marcus is always as cool as a cucumber whenever we visit. He had no qualms about handing over the van. And don't forget we think it was used in the robbery of the late shop, a shooting in broad daylight and the possible hit and run of Alfie Lovell."

"Like you say, playing it cool."

"No, Tom, I don't think Marcus has anything to do with this. Lena perhaps, Mark too, but not their son."

"Who then? Barton for the trainers, and somehow acquiring the two watches and a few dozen bags and passing them onto Knowles?"

Ruth nodded. "I can go with that."

"We still have the murders — Noah, Knowles, and Barton himself. At whose feet do we lay those?" he said.

Ruth understood the problem but she was no nearer solving it than Calladine was. "Knowles's lock up, then back to the station. See what forensics and Alice have turned up."

* * *

The lock-up was only round the corner. Ruth parked up, and they got out of the car only to come face to face with Ken Lovell, on his way to his store next door.

"I've hit a problem," he said. "I need another roll of that paper, but my supplier won't have it until tomorrow."

Just what Calladine didn't want to hear. He had been hoping to reclaim his home after today. "No worries, Ken. It's not the end of the world. While you're here, did you have much to do with Rob Knowles?"

"No, he were a crook, a loser. He should have told that Barton where to go but he didn't have the backbone. Now look what's happened, the man's been killed."

"Barton came here, to see Knowles?" Calladine asked.

"All the time. He brought him stuff to sell on his stall. Those trainers for instance. I knew at once they were knock-off. Expensive brand, not market fodder at all. I had a go at telling Rob but he weren't having any."

"Did you ever hear them argue?" Ruth asked.

"No, not much. Barton dropped stuff off late at night though. That got on my nerves if I was here. Back and forth up this alleyway in that bloody van of his. And then there was all that noise and shouting the other night, though that wasn't down to Barton. It were two big blokes, never seen them before. They drove a similar van to Barton."

"Can you recall exactly what night?" Ruth asked.

"Thursday, late on. I was in my lock-up sorting out what I needed for your sitting room." He nodded at Calladine. "I admit I'm no hero. I locked the door and hid behind those boxes over there until it all went quiet." Lovell gave them a sheepish look. "I could have helped him but I held back. What does that make me?"

"Sensible," Ruth said. "We believe the men who took Rob were killers. They wouldn't have hesitated when it came to silencing you."

"Do you have any idea what state Knowles was in when he was taken?" Calladine asked.

"He were still alive, shouting and screaming the odds. They must have taken him off in the van and that was the last I saw of him."

Calladine smiled. "Thanks, Ken, that could be helpful. We're just going to have a last look round, see if we've missed anything."

Ken Lovell left them to it.

"Shame I've got nothing to tell him about his son. I'd like nothing better than to give the man some closure," Calladine said.

"Come on," Ruth said. "Let's get this over."

The pair went inside and Calladine flicked on the light. There was still stock left, most of it littering the floor, but the designer bags had been taken away by forensics.

Ruth picked up a child's toy. "This lot is rubbish, so is the rest of the stuff left lying about."

Calladine had taken himself off to the far end of the unit and was searching through a pair of metal cabinets. "There's nothing interesting here either. I'm telling you, Ruth, we need something positive or we'll have Greco and the super on our backs."

"Not Greco's style as a rule. He usually keeps out of our cases unless he has to get involved."

Calladine had to agree. Greco was the best senior officer they'd had in a while. "I suppose it could be worse. We could have Birch back. Remind me to ask forensics what they got from this place. Given what Lovell just told us, whoever took Knowles must have left some trace."

But Ruth wasn't listening. She'd scooped up a crumpled piece of paper from the floor and was trying to decipher it. She turned it round in her hands before finally realising what it was. "I think they did, Tom. Look at this."

It was a hand-drawn map but it had been trampled on by any number of feet and the detail was almost obliterated. Calladine glanced at it over her shoulder. "It's the route up the M6 to the M62 and then on to the Leesworth junction."

Ruth turned the paper over. "There's more, look. It continues with the route from the Leesworth junction to . . ." She could hardly believe her eyes. She passed it to Calladine. "What d'you make of that?"

"I'd like to know how it got here."

"Possibly dropped or discarded by whoever took Knowles. You can see where the route leads. Now d'you see what I was getting at? You really shouldn't be so keen to trust people."

CHAPTER FORTY-FIVE

Before returning to station the pair made a short detour to the Duggan. Calladine was anxious to get the piece of paper into Julian's hands as soon as possible.

"We got one set of unidentified prints from Knowles's lock-up when we blitzed the place but they're not clear. Whoever left them must have realised their mistake and tried to wipe them off. But we're in luck." Julian gave them one of his rare smiles. "The prints were on the inside of the main door which had recently been painted, making it good and shiny. Whoever tried to obliterate the prints did so with a hankie perhaps, and wiped it over the surface."

"How does that help?" Ruth asked.

"I've done a swab and found saliva. They must have tried to wet it before the wiped the prints. I should have the DNA sequence shortly. If I'm right, it shouldn't belong to Knowles."

Ruth pulled a face. "Someone spat on a hankie and wiped it over the door. I've been in that lock-up, heaven knows what I touched."

Julian wasn't listening, he had his eyes on the piece of paper she had given him. "We missed that drawing during our search, a serious error and I apologise. But on the positive side, there's all sorts of detritus on this."

"Do the best you can. We need a result and quick," Calladine urged.

"Incidentally, the ballistics report on those bullets is in," Julian said. "The bullets that killed Knowles and Barton are the same as in the killings Dawlish gave you details about. This case would seem to cover a large geographic area."

The outcome from ballistics was what Calladine had expected. "Anything on the bullet in Kitty's wall?"

"Fired from Barton's rifle," Julian said.

That didn't surprise him either. They hurried out to the car.

"Where now? The station, or do you want to tackle you know who?" Ruth asked.

"Before we tackle him I want more evidence — the forensics Julian is working on, provided they give us the anticipated results. I want a cast iron case against that young man before we pounce."

"Station it is then," Ruth said.

※ ※ ※

Both Rocco and Alice were busy in the main office, Alice on the phone and Rocco with paperwork.

"I've got something, sir," Alice called to Calladine when she saw him. "The report is in on that mobile you found in Barton's bedroom. It didn't make sense so I was just checking the result with the Duggan."

"There's a lot about this case that hasn't made sense, Alice," Calladine said drily. "But before you report back, there's something I want to tell you all." He nodded to the uniformed officer at the back of the room to close the door. "We now have a prime suspect. Certain information has come to light and is currently getting the once over from Professor Batho. Providing it doesn't throw up any surprises, we hope to arrest Ricky Spooner later today."

At that there was a general buzz around the room as the team all started to talk at once.

"Want us to bring him in, sir?" Rocco asked.

Calladine looked as if he was only half listening. Something had struck him — the snippet of conversation so important to the case that he hadn't registered at the time.

"When I last spoke to Spooner he mentioned the bags. How could he know about them if he wasn't involved? He can't claim that Noah told him, they were only stolen a few days ago."

"So that's what you couldn't remember, well, thank goodness you have now," Ruth said. "But as for being evidence, it's still just his word against yours that the conversation ever happened. And evidence is crucial in this case. Spooner's legal people are top notch."

Ruth was right but his mood had lightened. Trying to recall what had been said, what he couldn't bring to mind, had been bugging him and this was a weight off.

"Sir," Alice called to him. "What I've discovered might help in the interim. That mobile I mentioned earlier, it was an unregistered pay as you go and must have been paid for with cash, but I doubt it belonged to Barton. The only prints on it were Ricky Spooner's."

Given what they now knew, that didn't surprise Calladine at all. "Which begs the question, what was it doing in Barton's bedroom? Any ideas?"

Ruth nudged him. "Barton's mother told us that her son and Spooner had come to blows, fighting in the street, remember. Maybe Spooner lost the phone then and Barton picked it up."

That was a possibility, but however Barton had come by the phone Calladine intended to use the information to his advantage. "Alice, the mobile was used to call a single number if I recall. Find out who it belongs to."

Alice gave him a big smile. "Already done, sir. The number was also that of a pay as you go and unregistered. But I used a tactic you've used in the past. I rang it."

"Good work, Alice. Who answered?"

"They didn't give a name, just grunted a response then swore when I said nothing. But it pinged a mast within metres of HMP Manchester."

Calladine knew what that meant — Mark Goddard. "Rocco, take a couple of uniformed officers and bring Spooner in and, Ruth, go and give our leader the good news."

CHAPTER FORTY-SIX

Calladine went to his office and sat down. He needed a minute. For days now all he'd wanted was a breakthrough, and now he had one his head was struggling to keep up. He would never have imagined that Spooner could be in league with Goddard. He'd thought the young man was merely on the periphery of the case. It would appear he'd got that very wrong. What he couldn't work out was why Goddard hadn't used someone he knew, someone from his old team. The other big question — did Lena know?

DCI Stephen Greco interrupted his thoughts. "You've made good progress. Just what we needed."

"I need to go to HMP Manchester and see Mark Goddard," Calladine said. "He's involved in this. If he'll talk, his testament will be useful."

"How likely is that?"

That was the big question, and Calladine had no real idea. Goddard could dig his heels in, refuse to say anything, which wouldn't help the case one bit.

"You put the man away," Greco reminded him. "Why not let someone else do the visit, someone he doesn't know?"

Calladine's head shot up. "You?"

Greco nodded. "It makes sense. Meanwhile, assemble everything you can on Spooner's involvement in the case and face him with it. He's a young man. If he believes it's likely he'll be locked away for a good many years, he might talk. Armed with his testimony I tackle Goddard. Pit one villain against the other and see who cracks first."

Calladine was reluctant to give up any part of the case to Greco but he knew what he'd put to him made sense. If Calladine turned up at the prison it'd only antagonise Goddard and he'd be unlikely to get anywhere.

"Okay, that's fine with me. Spooner is being brought in and we should have further forensic evidence later today."

Greco nodded. "I'll get the visit organised for tomorrow, then."

As soon as Greco had left, Ruth rapped on Calladine's door. "Fancy something to eat? We've not stopped all day and it isn't over yet. Rocco's picked up Spooner and they're on their way in."

"I'm not hungry," he said.

"What about Kitty? You should tell her you'll be late."

"I don't think she cares anymore. She stays at her own place mostly these days." He sighed and looked at the pile of files on his desk. "It's my work that's changed things, I know it is. She was fine while I was at home."

"D'you like her?"

Calladine knew what Ruth was getting at. "Not enough to give up the job, and she knows it, I'm afraid."

"Playing second fiddle to your job is what's put paid to all of your romances so far, Tom. One day you will have to choose."

Not something he wanted to think about. "Anything come through from forensics yet?"

"I'm just about to ring them. The DNA stuff will take a little longer but any fingerprints on the map should be through quick enough. Oh, and Dawlish is back. He's looking particularly pleased with himself."

* * *

Jeff Dawlish had completed his search of the Northern Sportswear stock and was back in the main office. "It's as we thought," he told Calladine. "Dozens of boxes of the new line, taped up, looking the business, but all they contained was old lines fit only for the sales. Riley must have known. In order to keep it a secret he filled the empty boxes and hoped the problem would be solved before the launch day."

"That'll be why he hired a private detective," Calladine said. "He was hoping to get his stock back before it came to light."

"If he'd reported the theft earlier, the entire case might have turned out different."

He might have a point. The theft of the trainers had been opportunistic on Barton's part, and then when the chance to steal the watches and the bags from wherever Spooner was hiding them also presented itself, he jumped at it.

Dawlish grinned. "If an arrest is imminent, I'll fight you for him. I've seen the ballistics report, we're after the same crew. He was joking, but Calladine knew damn well he meant it. But there was no way that was happening. Spooner and whoever else was involved in this were his.

CHAPTER FORTY-SEVEN

Spooner was brought to the station, processed, and seated in an interview room to wait. Within ten minutes he was mouthing off to the uniformed officer watching him.

"Look, moron, it's getting late and I haven't had my tea yet. How much longer is this going to take?"

"DI Calladine will be with you soon," the officer said.

"Him again. What does he want me for now? I thought we'd sorted everything, and it was all cool between us."

As he was speaking, Calladine entered the room with Ruth. "Things change, Ricky," Calladine said, "particularly where crime is concerned. And not always for the better."

Ricky Spooner flushed and his eyes darted from one detective to the other. "Solicitor?"

"If you wish. The officer here will arrange for you to make the call and we'll return when you're ready."

Calladine and Ruth left the interview room. "How long is this going to take?" Ruth asked.

"It can take all night as far as I'm concerned. I want to nail the bastard. He's got away with everything so far, but not any more." He looked across the room at Alice. "Get the Duggan for me."

"You sure this is our man?" Dawlish asked.

"Yes, but until I get the forensics I can't prove it. Currently I'm going with my gut, a chance remark he made and a couple of unexplained items. One being a roughly drawn map and the other a mobile phone found in Barton's bedroom."

Dawlish didn't look too impressed with that. He stood up, grabbed his jacket, and made for the door. "I'll leave you to it. Late shifts don't suit me. This is your end of the case anyway. I'll read the reports in the morning."

"Riley must have worn him out," Ruth joked once he'd left. "But he has a point, it is getting late."

"Go home if you need to, Ruth. Rocco can do the interview with me."

Ruth shook her head. "No, that wouldn't be fair. Besides, I wouldn't mind a crack at Spooner myself."

Calladine made them both a strong coffee and went over to the window. The weather had been warm and sunny but now it'd started to rain. "Spooner's brief is smart. If there's any way he can get him released, he'll find it."

"Once Julian comes up with the goods we'll have solid evidence. There's nothing even the cleverest of lawyers can do about that."

"Greco is visiting Goddard tomorrow but I doubt he'll get much from him. He has no reason to help us. We're in no position to cut any sort of deal."

"Greco speaks to him and he'll know we've arrested Spooner. Goddard has no idea what Spooner will tell us. He might play ball if only to lay the blame squarely at Spooner's feet."

"That's what Greco is banking on too, playing one of them off against the other."

"If it gets us what we want, why not?" Ruth smiled. "Spooner is the weak link here. He thinks Goddard has spoken to us and he'll be desperate to tell us what we need to know in order to shift the blame."

Calladine's mobile rang. It was the Duggan. "Come on, Julian, cheer me up."

"Your voice sounds strained. That means you're working too hard, Tom. Remember, it's not good for you."

"I'll take it easy when this one's done."

"The paper with the drawing of the map. There were two sets of prints on it. One set belonged to Spooner and the other to a man called Ronald Bailey. He's done time, up until six months ago he was in HMP Manchester."

"Same as one of our prime suspects, Mark Goddard," Calladine said.

"Everything you need is on the system," Julian said. "He often works with his brother, Robert. Both are in their late forties, heavily built and from what I read, devoid of scruples."

Possibly the two 'burly' men that had been referred to. "The other set, Julian. You're sure they belong to Spooner?"

"Yes, as do the prints on the mobile phone Barton had in his bedroom."

"You have the original drawing, email a copy. I'll need it for the interview. And thanks, the forensics we've got will help enormously."

He finished the call and turned to Ruth. "When that drawing comes through, get it printed out. I bet Spooner's face will be a picture when he sees it."

"The map leads directly to his showroom, Tom. I know it covers a large area, far more land than they need for car sales. I can't recall exactly but I'm sure Spooners' own some outbuildings at the back. We should get a warrant and have them checked out."

"Good call." He checked his watch. "I'll speak to Greco and see if we can't do something this evening."

CHAPTER FORTY-EIGHT

Within the hour Spooner's solicitor, Clive Collymore, arrived not looking too pleased at having been called out. Calladine and Ruth entered the interview room and sat opposite the pair. After the introductions for the tape, the solicitor said, "I do hope this isn't another waste of time, Inspector. You've spoken to my client once already and nothing came of that."

"I can assure you that this interview is crucial. New evidence has come to light." Calladine smiled at them both before turning to Spooner. "You and I have already had a long chat, Ricky. But remind me, what d'you know about the theft of the trainers, watches, and handbags, some of which were found in Knowles's lock-up."

Spooner shrugged. "Nothing."

"And you're quite sure?"

"Look, this is wearing a bit thin now. Why pick on me? I know nothing about any thefts," Spooner said.

"What about the murders then?" Calladine asked. "What d'you know about them?"

"Are you off your head or something? I've never killed anyone."

"Perhaps not, but you know people who have." Calladine took the copy of the map from the file and placed it in front of the pair. "Tell me about the drawing, Ricky."

"Nothing to do with me."

"One side shows the motorway system from Birmingham to the Leesworth junction on the M62. On the reverse is a detailed map from the junction to your showroom." He gave the young man a moment to consider this. "How d'you explain that?"

"I can't. All I can suggest is that someone else drew the map, for a customer perhaps," Spooner said.

"I don't agree. I think it's directions for two men, Ronald and Robert Bailey, who brought a container full of stolen goods north with the intention of storing them at your premises."

At the mention of those names Spooner's face was indeed a picture. He turned to his brief, frantic for some nugget that would make it right. But the lawyer remained silent. Finally, Spooner said, "You're mad, you've finally flipped. That's a ridiculous idea."

Ignoring the comment, Calladine asked, "Have you ever seen this map before, Ricky?"

"No, of course I haven't. It has absolutely nothing to do with me."

"I don't believe you."

Spooner shrugged again. "Please yourself but I'm telling the truth."

"This is a copy of one that was found in Rob Knowles's lock-up. The original has been with forensics most of the day and has your fingerprints all over it. Given what you've just told me, how d'you explain that?"

Spooner's eyes widened. He turned to his solicitor. "It's a set up. I don't even know that man and I've certainly never been to his lock-up."

Next, Calladine showed them a photo of the mobile found in Barton's bedroom.

"That's not mine, Inspector," Spooner said.

"Again, your prints are all over it, no one else's, and it's being tested for your DNA. What happened, lose it in a fight with Barton? Or perhaps he stole it from you."

"I don't know, I can't remember."

"You see, Ricky, the mobile is interesting because it was used to ring one number only. Want to tell me whose number that is?"

Spooner glared at both detectives. "This is rubbish. You won't make it stick. I've done nothing."

"When did you first contact Mark Goddard?" Ruth asked. "Or perhaps he contacted you. Have an interesting proposition for you, did he?"

On hearing the name, the solicitor looked uneasy. "Can I have a word with my client?"

"Certainly. We'll resume the interview in the morning."

"Does that mean I can go?" Spooner asked.

Calladine shook his head. "I'm afraid not. You'll stay with us until our enquires are complete. Speak to your lawyer, use the time wisely, Ricky, and heed the advice you're given. Think carefully about what you tell us next. Goddard is a hardened criminal and is already serving a long sentence. He has nothing to lose."

CHAPTER FORTY-NINE

There was a note from Alice on Calladine's desk. It had been too late to organise the warrant today but it was scheduled for first thing in the morning. That was okay, with luck the DNA results would be in by then too.

"We might as well call it a day," he said.

"Will Kitty be at yours? This case is enough on your plate without the added burden of personal problems. The pair of you need to talk and you look as if you could do with the company," Ruth said.

"Kitty's not my biggest fan at the moment. The Amy problem has obviously touched a nerve."

"I don't blame her. Amy is still fond of you and doesn't do anything to hide it." Ruth shook her head. "You're looking a bit pale and tired. Are you sure you wouldn't be better coming to mine for a bite to eat?"

"I'm not a child, Ruth, I'm more than capable of taking care of myself. Anyway, you've already fed me once this week. I'll be okay."

She smiled. "As long as you're sure. Any problems, you know where I am. See you bright and early in the morning."

Calladine watched her go. She waved from the door and he heard her footsteps on the wooden floor of the corridor as she walked away. He didn't like the fussing but nonetheless he appreciated her concern. She'd been his rock over the years, the one person he could not do this job without. Suddenly he felt vulnerable, the words 'old' and 'past it' flew into his mind, instantly depressing him. The years were passing and like it not, sooner or later he'd have to consider both his health and his future. Regardless of what Ruth might think, he needed a whisky or two. The Wheatsheaf it was then.

He gathered his things, left the station, and crossed the road heading for the pub. He ordered a single malt and stood at the bar. The first went nowhere, the second just about touched the sides. He was about to order a third when someone spoke from behind him.

"Thought you'd jacked all that in."

Calladine spun round to be faced with Doc Hoyle. "It's just a quick one, to wash the day away, you know."

Sebastian Hoyle shook his head. "No need to explain to me, Tom. I know the pressures only too well. But you do need to take care of yourself. A fright is one thing but we're both of an age when the worst can happen."

Calladine set the glass down hard on the counter and grimaced. "We're dealing with a complex case, I've been away and I've found diving straight back into the thick of it hard."

The doc nodded. "Remember when I had that back trouble? I took time off. When I returned to the job I was just the same as you. I realised there was more to life than wall to wall work. That was when I decided to retire from pathology and do something lighter."

Calladine laughed. "Ruth found you still hard at it in A&E the other day — that's lighter, is it?"

"Part time, Tom. I virtually choose my own hours. The pressure's gone and I enjoy it."

"I have to say, you look a lot better than you did, much slimmer too."

Doc Hoyle tapped him on the shoulder. "Think about it. Less hours, lose the pressure. It could work for you too."

He meant it, Calladine could see. "The thought had crossed my mind," he admitted. "But then I think about the team, especially Ruth, and I know I can't go through with it."

"Ruth would understand. After all, she's ambitious. She could get that leg up to inspector she so badly wants."

Calladine shot him a look. "Has she told you that?"

"Not in so many words, but it's obvious. Ruth is a good detective and like the rest of us, she's not getting any younger. If she is to make inspector it will have to be soon."

Doc Hoyle had given him something to think about. Retirement was an uncomfortable concept and not something Calladine wanted imminently, but it had to be considered.

He walked home, his chat with the doc still on his mind. Turning onto his street he met Ryan with Sam. The dog barked, pulling on the lead in an effort to get to him.

Ryan grinned. "He's missed you. But we've had a good time. A long walk and his favourite tea."

Calladine took the lead from him. "Thanks, I owe you."

"I'll sort him in the morning if you want," the lad offered.

"Yes, please, that would be great. I've got an early start."

Calladine reached his front door. There were no lights on so Kitty wasn't there. He patted the dog. "Looks like another microwave dinner."

CHAPTER FIFTY

Tuesday

Calladine was up and about by six the next morning. He'd slept fitfully, his mind rarely still, various details about the case flitting in and out of his consciousness.

The main event of today was the search of the outbuilding at the rear of the Spooner showroom premises. After which they would resume the interview with Ricky. Calladine hoped that a night under lock and key would have made him more willing to cooperate.

He left the house at seven, dropping Sam and a packet of his favourite dog food off with Ryan. "I might be late, depends on how the day goes. If it's a bother just say, I won't mind."

"We'll be fine, no worries. I've got college this afternoon but my mum's here and she'll look after him."

Domestic arrangements sorted, Calladine drove to the station. He could see Ruth's car already parked up. "You're the early bird," he said.

"That's what having a toddler in the house does for you. Greco's asked for a word. He came bustling in here earlier all red faced and looking like he had the worries of the world on his shoulders. Whatever's bothering him must be serious."

Calladine had no idea what that might be. All he wanted now was a steady walk to the end of this — get the evidence to put paid to Spooner's villainy and to find the Bailey brothers. He hurried along the corridor and rapped on Greco's office door.

"We have a problem, Tom," Greco began, nodding for him to sit down. As usual Greco's office was immaculate, not a thing out of place and all the items on his desk carefully arranged. "Mark Goddard was found dead in his cell this morning. The prison medic is going with a heart attack. Apparently, Goddard had a faulty valve and other problems. To be absolutely sure I've asked Dr Barrington to do an autopsy. She will report back before lunch today."

It was the last thing Calladine had been expecting and he was shocked. Goddard was a villain with a horrendous reputation for violence, a perfect candidate for organising the killings in Leesworth. But perhaps he was wrong. If his death wasn't down to a heart attack, then someone had got to him, but why? "That puts paid to the interview then. We could have done with his input too."

"Input I strongly suspect a third party did not want him to give," Greco said. "I find the entire episode far too convenient. It will suit Spooner to have Goddard out of the way, unable to spill his guts to us in order to save his own skin."

"You think Spooner had him got at?" Calladine asked. "But how could he do that? He was here, locked up. Apart from which, I'm not sure that Spooner wields that much influence. He's a young man, Stephen, twenty-four years old with no history of violence."

"There are the two heavies, the Bailey brothers," Greco reminded him. "They are more than capable. We need to find them, bring the pair in without delay."

"We have circulated their descriptions and photos. We're hopeful it won't be long." Calladine paused for a moment. Was Greco right about the Baileys? Had they somehow managed to have Goddard killed? If so, how?

Greco handed Calladine an envelope. "The warrant for the car showroom. Let's hope the search bears fruit. What d'you intend to do about Dawlish?"

"If he's not here I can't include him, can I?" He smiled. "I'll let Rocco lead on this and join him once I've had a word with Lena Goddard."

"No, get Rocco to contact Dawlish first and take him along. This is his case too, Tom."

Calladine went back to the main office and told the team what had happened.

"Murder, sir?" Rocco asked.

"I'll be surprised if it isn't and Greco thinks the same. You are to lead the search of Spooner's showroom and take Dawlish with you. Our leader's instructions, not mine."

"He's okay actually, sir. Easy to get on with. So who knew Goddard was to be interviewed?"

Calladine considered the question and what it meant. "Apart from us, only Spooner and his solicitor."

"One of them, in that case."

Everything was so cut and dried in Rocco's world — oh that it was that simple. "Spooner's mobile was taken from him when he was arrested," Ruth said. "He's been sitting in a cell all night, so realistically that only leaves his brief."

Calladine knew the lawyer belonged to one of the most successful firms in the area. He was the senior partner. Despite that, he had to be the weak link. He turned to Alice. "His name is Clive Collymore, do some digging, see what you can find."

Ruth sighed. "We're thinking he's bent now, are we?"

"Either that or one of us tipped off whoever did for Goddard. Before we join the showroom search I think we should have a word with Lena, get her take on this."

"Very brave of you, given your history."

"I want to test the mood, Ruth. See for myself how the news has affected both Lena and her son."

"You have a theory?" she asked.

"Not really, it's more me clutching at straws again."

CHAPTER FIFTY-ONE

Goddard's garden centre was open as usual, which Calladine found odd considering what had happened. He spotted a couple of new faces among the workforce, replacements for Noah and Barton no doubt. Calladine made his way to the office where he hoped to find Marcus. Ruth held back to answer a call on her mobile.

As soon as he entered he heard the familiar voice. "What the hell d'you want? You're not welcome here. I thought I made myself clear last time. Can't you take a hint?"

"We've come to offer our condolences," he said calmly, "and to ask you about Mark's health these last few years."

"He had a heart condition, as you must realise now, given what's happened. Shame he didn't get better care from the medics in that prison. I did tell Mark to complain. If he had, he might still be alive."

"Is Marcus here?"

"No, he's taken the day off, he's far too upset to work."

Calladine nodded. That seemed reasonable enough. "You can't be too happy yourself."

She shrugged. "Someone has to keep the place running. If not Marcus, then that falls to me. I was told you lot planned to visit Mark today. What was that about?"

"Our current case. We thought he might be able to help."

Lena laughed. "Mark help you? In your dreams, Calladine."

"It might have been in his interest to tell us the truth about certain robberies and three murders."

"Robbery? Murder? Are you mad? The man has been locked up for years. No way can you lay something like that at his feet."

"He has the right contacts, Lena, and plenty of people on the outside to do his dirty work for him."

"You're off your head, you are. The man's dead, let him rest in peace." She turned her back on him and stormed off.

"Wait for me," Ruth called out, running after him. "You'll want to hear this."

Calladine nodded towards the car. "We might as well be going, we'll get nothing here."

"I'm not so sure," she said with a smile. "That was Alice on the phone. She did that digging you wanted and hit gold."

"She's a clever cop is our Alice."

Ruth nodded. "She is. Well, for the last two years Lena Goddard has been having an affair with Clive Collymore, Spooner's solicitor. So serious is it that he's left his wife and is getting a divorce."

Calladine gave her a beaming smile. This could be useful. "Lena and Collymore, eh. An odd pairing. Is she sure?"

"Yes, and I'm trying to work out what it means, how it helps the case."

"It means that Collymore must have told the wrong person about Mark's impending interview. Mark must have known something Lena didn't want us to find out. She's a strong woman, clever too. I always thought her the brains behind Mark Goddard's operation. If Mark is no longer any use to her, she wouldn't hesitate to give her affection to someone who would be, and to get rid of Mark if he became a liability."

"You think she's using Collymore?" Ruth asked.

Calladine nodded. "Very much so. I suspect she's the brains behind this operation too. Spooner's involved merely as a storage facility. He's an unlikely partner in crime for a woman like Lena."

"That doesn't explain her interest in Collymore," Ruth pointed out.

Calladine took his mobile from his jacket pocket and rang Alice. "Do something for me. Find out who represented Mark Goddard the last time he tried for parole." He turned to Ruth. "Greco is arranging for the Duggan to do Goddard's PM. I know he's asked Natasha to report back asap but let's get down there ourselves, see what she comes up with."

They'd no sooner reached their car when Alice rang back. "Collymore was Goddard's brief, sir, but only for the first few weeks and then Goddard dismissed him. I have a contact at the courts, my cousin, so I asked him. He said the pair had a falling out. Apparently Collymore advised him to plead guilty but Goddard refused. He also said that all through the trial Collymore and Lena were inseparable."

"Thanks, Alice. Get anything else, let me know at once." What she'd discovered was interesting and it would explain Lena and Collymore's relationship, but what about the leak of information about Mark's impending interview? What were they afraid the villain would disclose?

CHAPTER FIFTY-TWO

Calladine and Ruth pulled into the Duggan car park. "Once we've finished here we'll have a word with Collymore," Calladine said. "See what his take is on this."

"He's got to be as bent as Lena, surely," Ruth said.

"Possibly." The truth was Calladine wasn't so sure. If Mark Goddard had become obstructive in any way, would Lena have had him killed? The picture the pair painted of their relationship over the years was of a solid partnership, but now that was in doubt. Goddard's death at this very moment was far too convenient. It suited Spooner, they'd no one else's take on events other than his, but who else would benefit? As far as Calladine could work out, if not Mark that only left whoever was the brains behind the thefts and the killings. Could that be Lena? Did she have Mark killed because he would tell the police as much to save his skin?

"I didn't realise you were attending," Natasha said. "I'm afraid I've already started. He's an interesting one. I can confirm it wasn't a heart attack that killed him. His cardiac problems have been well documented over the years by the prison doctors. There are scans and so on and he was prescribed drugs. They would have been happy to chalk it up as such if DCI Greco hadn't insisted."

"Did the prison appear bothered by the prospect of a post mortem in any way?"

"No, but the doctor I spoke to on the phone did say we were wasting our time and taxpayers' money. He thought it was all cut and dried."

"If not his heart, what did do for him then?" Ruth asked.

"An overdose of morphine," Natasha said, surprising them both. "There's no trace in his stomach, so it had to have been administered straight into his bloodstream."

"Someone injected him. You're sure?" Calladine asked.

Natasha gave him a look. "That's why I'm holding this magnifying glass. I'm currently scrutinising the body to find the injection site."

"Any luck?"

"Nothing so far. The dose was off the scale, so it was definitely intended to kill. This is murder, Tom. We were just supposed to reach for his medical notes and attribute his death to a heart attack."

"If his demise hadn't been so convenient for someone we're currently holding, we might have done just that." Calladine smiled. "But as it is, both Greco and me are suspicious buggers and want the truth."

"Found it," Natasha cried. "Will you look at that!" She pointed to a patch of skin between two of Goddard's toes. "I would have missed it if it wasn't for the redness. The man had an allergic reaction and the site is swollen and inflamed."

"Murder then?"

Natasha turned and looked at Calladine. "Most definitely. I'll write the report shortly. DCI Greco has asked for it urgently."

"Thanks, Natasha, you've confirmed what we all suspected."

"Who do we suspect for this one?" Ruth asked as they left the building.

"Not Spooner. He was banged up and didn't make any calls after we interviewed him. The only other person who knew we wanted to speak to Goddard was Collymore."

"Such a highly respected solicitor? You think him capable of murder?"

"No, but he might have let it slip to Lena, not understanding the importance of the information."

"Is it important?"

"Yes, Ruth. I believed Spooner was in cahoots with Mark and the Bailey brothers. My plan was to lean on Mark and get him to give us something to implicate Spooner. We would use that information to frighten Spooner into telling us the truth to save his own skin."

"We've got plenty on Spooner as it is," she said.

"A scribbled map which any half decent lawyer would explain away in court."

"There's Barton's mobile."

"Could have been planted, Ruth."

"But Mark might just have dug his heels in and said nothing."

"Or he could have told us something we weren't expecting, something that implicated Lena for instance."

Ruth stopped in her tracks. "You're suggesting that the thefts and killings are not down to Mark Goddard but Lena?"

"Yes, which is why she didn't want us talking to him. We get heavy, Mark thinks whatever we've got will add yet more time to his sentence and he'll fight back."

"Want to bring her in?" she asked.

"First, I want another word with Spooner. He thinks we're after Mark. I want to see his reaction when he learns the man is dead."

CHAPTER FIFTY-THREE

Back at the station the pair grabbed a quick coffee before speaking to Spooner. Alice was still hard at work on her computer and Rocco was out searching Spooner's showroom.

"Feel free to interrupt the minute Rocco reports in," Calladine told Alice. "Anything else on the two lovebirds?"

"Collymore left his wife six months ago and has taken an apartment in Hopecross."

Calladine shook his head. "Silly man. When this comes to light, his association with Lena Goddard will be the death knell for his career."

He picked up the file from his desk. "Right, let's get to it. I want this one wrapping up."

Ricky Spooner looked tired and dishevelled. He was sitting with a man they hadn't seen before who Calladine took to be the duty solicitor.

Spooner scowled at the two detectives and banged his fist on the table. "You've no right treating me like this."

"No Mr Collymore this morning?" Calladine asked.

"He cried off. This is someone you lot got for me," Spooner said.

"Barry Holt. And if I was you, Mr Spooner, I'd moderate my behaviour," the solicitor said.

"Don't tell me what to do," yelled Spooner.

"Mark Goddard has been murdered," Calladine began. "And him safely behind bars too." He tutted. "Just goes to show, no one's safe, not even in prison."

He could see that his words had rattled Spooner. The young man's eyes widened and he let out a gasp. "Nothing to do with me."

"It's got everything to do with you, Ricky. You see, Lena didn't want us speaking to him, afraid of what he might tell us. She's not a nice woman is our Lena. She has no more use for someone and — well, poor Mark."

At the mention of Lena's name Spooner started to shake. "You . . . you have to protect me. You don't know what she's like."

"Oh but I do. I know Lena of old and I know exactly what she is like." He paused, watching Spooner take a gulp of his water. "Want to tell me how she ensnared you? How you came to work for her? It will go better for your case, Ricky, if you help us. Right now Lena is frightened and that makes her one dangerous woman. I think she's cleaning up, making sure there's no one left who can cause trouble for her down the line. I know how ruthless she is, clever too, which is why Mark was behind bars and not her."

Spooner looked as if he was about to faint. He swallowed more water and then looked Calladine straight in the eye. "Okay. I'm sick of this, it's not worth the hassle, none of it is."

He was going to tell them. This was exactly what Calladine had been hoping for.

"I did it for the money," Spooner began. "She's paying me a fortune to store some stock they can't keep at the garden centre. I'm a soft touch where dosh is concerned, I told you that before."

True, he did, the problem he had with the trainers had also been down to his greed. "Some stuff, that's what she told you? Did you take a look at it?"

"None of my business. It arrives, I store it and then it gets taken away. A doddle and very lucrative," Spooner said.

"What do you think it is, this stock?"

Spooner shrugged. "Like she said, stuff they can't keep at the centre. I wasn't that concerned to be honest."

"Who makes the deliveries?" Calladine asked.

"Couple of big blokes. I don't get into a discussion with them or anything, just tell them where to store the goods."

"What about picking the stuff up? What happens then?"

"Always at night but the same blokes," Spooner said.

"How long do you store the stuff for?" Calladine asked.

Spooner shrugged. "It varies but two weeks tops."

Now for the big question. "Have you any idea where the stuff was going?"

"Not really, but a couple of times one of the blokes rang to check the ferry times from Hull."

That was why, apart from what was in Knowles's lock-up, none of these goods had surfaced for sale. "If it's on its way to a ferry in Hull it's hardly garden centre stock, is it?" Calladine said. "D'you know any names, Ricky?"

Spooner shook his head.

At that point Alice entered the room and asked to have a word with Calladine.

They went out to the corridor. "The search paid off. There's a large outbuilding to the rear of the showroom. Rocco said it was well locked up but he's managed to get it open." She smiled. "The space inside was stuffed to the gills with designer goods — handbags, jewellery, and a host of other stuff."

"Good work. Get some bodies down there and match up the goods with Dawlish's lists of stolen property."

Calladine went back into the interview room. "There's quite a haul in that building behind your showroom. Does your mother know?"

"No," Spooner insisted. "She only ever ventures as far as the office. The rest of it she leaves to me."

"I think your store was broken into and stuff stolen. Want to tell me about that?" Calladine was thinking about the watches and handbags. "Certain items turned up on Rob Knowles's market stall."

"That was down to Barton. He stole my keys and copied them. He took a load of stuff and left me to carry the can. I was terrified. Lena was livid and demanded to know what happened. I had no choice, it was either tell her about Barton or suffer the consequences." He hung his head. "I reckon I signed his death warrant."

"You didn't kill him, Ricky. Those thugs Lena hired did that." Calladine gave him a moment to let that sink in. "We found a phone in Barton's bedroom. It belongs to you but has only ever been used to ring Mark Goddard. Why, if it's Lena who's running this?"

"She was using him too. Lena needed information from time to time and wanted him sweet. I did speak to him occasionally mostly to ask about suppliers."

Calladine could believe that. Lena couldn't know all Mark's old contacts.

"What happens now?" Spooner asked.

He was pale and tired looking. Calladine felt a flash of sympathy for him. "You'll be charged but things will be easier because you've helped us. An officer will take a statement shortly."

"Can I go then?"

"Apart from anything else, you're in danger, Ricky. For now you're safer with us."

"A lock and key didn't do much for Mark Goddard, did it?"

CHAPTER FIFTY-FOUR

Calladine returned to the main office happy with the way things had gone. "Spooner's talked," he announced, a smile on his face. "Now we go get Lena." He looked at Rocco. "Take a couple of uniforms and bring her in."

"What about Collymore?" Ruth asked

"We'll get round to him, don't worry."

"Sir!" Alice called out. "The Bailey brothers have been arrested in Hull."

"Arrange for them to be collected and brought to us. It looks like us and DI Dawlish's team will have to fight for them." Calladine grinned. Things were looking up.

"Where is Dawlish?" Ruth asked.

"He's been with Rocco, checking out the stolen goods at the showroom. He should be well pleased with the way things have turned out," Calladine said.

"We've sorted the designer stuff," Ruth said, "the trainers too after a fashion, but they're not part of the same case, are they? Lena had nothing to do with purloining them. That was down to Barton. What I don't understand is Noah Crosby's part in all this."

"Barton stole from Northern Sportwear and Spooner's outbuilding. I think the Bailey brothers did for him like they did Knowles, but as for poor Noah . . ." Still talking, Calladine wandered off towards the coffee corner and switched on the kettle. "I have a theory though."

"Want to let me in on it?" she asked.

"Let's get the Lena business wound up first, then I've got a couple of forensic tests to check on."

"Noah has to have been mixed up in this somewhere. He was pally with both Barton and Spooner," she said. "By the way, the lab has been on. The swab taken from Knowles's lock-up came from Ronald Bailey. The DNA checks out."

Calladine nodded. "A slip up when they went for Knowles, same as throwing away the drawing of the map. Very careless but helpful to us." He looked at the clock on the office wall. "I fancy some lunch, keep my strength up in readiness for tackling Lena."

"Canteen?" Ruth asked. "And you can tell me your theory about what happened to Noah. And don't forget the mark left on his skin. Got an explanation for that one?"

"It was found on Barton too when he was attacked, remember."

"Come on then, who d'you reckon?" she said.

"I need to talk to the suspect, and like I said check a few things, then I'll tell you."

Ruth frowned at him. "Don't go swanning off on your own and getting into trouble. You go tackling some secret killer, you take back-up."

Calladine smiled at her. "I'm not daft."

"Well I haven't a clue who you could be talking about and my brain is way past working it out. This case has been a horror from start to finish and no mistake."

"We're nearly done. We'll interview Lena and Collymore. I intend to leave the Bailey brothers to Dawlish. This was his case originally, after all."

The pair stood side by side studying the menu, watched by one of the canteen staff.

"Before you decide, the steak pie and the fish are off. It's way past lunch and they're always popular," she said.

"Can't think why," Ruth whispered to Calladine. God knows what they put in the pie but it's never looked like cow to me."

Calladine cast his eyes over the depleted hotplates. "They've got nowt. Fancy sending out for sandwiches instead?"

"I fancy a gin over the road but we're still working. Yeah, we'll get sarnies and prepare for Lena. She's not going to be happy."

"My heart bleeds."

CHAPTER FIFTY-FIVE

Lena Goddard was brought to the station, processed, and left to wait in an interview room with a uniformed officer. Ruth had been right, she wasn't happy. She spent the time pacing up and down the room, arms folded, and shouting the odds at everyone who came near, including the solicitor arranged for her.

Calladine could hear the commotion from outside the interview room. "Let's get this over with," he said to Ruth. "I'm tired of all the drama. The sooner Lena appreciates that this is the end of the road, the better."

"She's giving that young solicitor a roasting. She can't be happy with what he's proposing."

"It's Barry Holt again," Calladine said.

"He's a bit quiet, definitely not the pushy type. I doubt he'll suit Lena," Ruth said.

"Too bad. It's who she's got."

The pair entered the room and sat down opposite Holt. Lena was still pacing. She was angry, the hand holding the glass of water shook. Her expression was stony and she regarded him with hate. "You've got some front, Calladine. Arresting me is a big mistake. When this is over, I'm going to sue the arse off you."

"Sit down, Lena. The sooner we talk, the sooner it's over."

"And where's Clive? He's my solicitor, not this idiot."

Holt shuffled on his seat and cleared his throat. "The inspector will get you someone else if you're not satisfied with me."

"But not Collymore," Calladine said quickly. "He is also waiting to be interviewed, so he's unable to represent anyone."

That knocked the wind out of Lena. She sat down on her chair without further argument, as if she'd crumpled. "He has a heart condition. Don't upset him so he loses his temper. It's not good for him."

"A heart condition, like Mark?"

"Yes, that's what killed him."

"No, it wasn't. Mark was murdered."

Lena looked stunned. "How can you say that? His heart was ready to give out. Everyone at the prison knew about it."

"They might have done, but what killed him was an overdose of morphine. But then you'll know that."

Lena Goddard stared at Calladine, her face expressionless. "You're wrong. I didn't kill him. I've wanted to many times, I've had offers from people who wanted to help me but I've never been able to actually go through with it."

"Pull the other one, Lena."

"You sit there all high and mighty but you have no idea. It wasn't all bad, you know. There were good times and I did love Mark in my own way. I felt I had to protect him. No one tried harder than me to keep him out of prison."

"You can keep the lies coming for as long as you want, Lena. Collymore will tell us the truth. He's a lawyer, he knows better than to lie to us. He might even do a deal."

Lena lowered her eyes and shook her head. "Clive is a good man and I've ruined his reputation. His career is finished and all because he believed every word I told him. I never intended to continue Mark's business when he went inside but I had no choice."

"I take it you're not talking about the garden centre. You must mean the thieving of designer goods."

"Okay, Calladine, don't get clever with me," she snapped.

"When did you get involved with the Bailey brothers, Lena?"

"Mark's known them for years. I needed muscle, thugs not afraid to get their hands dirty."

Calladine grimaced. "And they got seriously dirty working for you. They're killers, the pair of them. They've left a trail of death and destruction the length of the country."

"I wasn't party to the killings," she said hastily. "I hate violence of any sort. They were supposed to just steal the goods and transport them to our storage facility."

"You didn't really expect those they robbed to simply stand by and let them take whatever they wanted, did you?"

"I didn't ask for details."

"You should have. They murdered people, Lena, anyone who stood in their way, and you were party to that, Mark too. By the storage facility, you mean the building at the back of Spooner's showroom, I suppose."

"We have nowhere at the centre, besides it would have been too dangerous, anyone could stumble on it. Spooner offered me a large building, convenient and cheap," she said.

"I can understand stealing all that high end stuff, but what were you doing with it?" Ruth asked her.

Lena turned her attention to Ruth and smiled evilly. "Enjoy your job, do you? Pay well?" She laughed. "I bet it doesn't. You've seen the stuff I deal in. How would you like to own one of those handbags for a fraction of the cost, or a piece of jewellery that would ordinarily have a price tag to match your annual salary?" Lena nodded. "I see from the expression on your face that you get it. We sell to middlemen who in turn move the stuff on. At the prices we're asking, we can barely keep up with demand."

"Middlemen where?" Ruth asked.

"This country and abroad." She looked at Calladine. "Check my desk in the office, there's an entire file's worth of names."

Calladine would do just that and then he'd pass the information on to Europol and all the forces around the UK who were involved. "You will make a statement and then be charged," he told her. "Apart from the thieving, you are a party to murder. Not only those connected to the robberies but that of your husband, Mark, too."

"Not Mark. I told you. You need to check that one again, Calladine."

He nodded to Ruth and the pair made to leave. "You'll be staying with us, Lena. If you want to speak to anyone, the desk sergeant will arrange it."

"And Clive? What about him?"

"None of your business."

This made her agitated and she got up from her seat. "He didn't know anything, I promise you. I made him tell me the details of your interview with Spooner, which is how I learned of your intention to interview Mark. Neither Clive nor I realised what the consequences would be."

"Didn't know you very well at all, did he, Lena?"

CHAPTER FIFTY-SIX

They went back along the corridor. "What will happen to Collymore?" Ruth asked.

"Depends on whether any evidence is found to link him to the robberies or murders. But having met him, I doubt there'll be anything. The man is besotted with Lena and didn't see past her winning smile."

The pair entered the main office to a huge cheer from the team. "Well done," Greco said. "It's a good result. The CPS are confident we have an excellent case against Lena Goddard and the Bailey brothers. They'll be charged with the murders of Crosby, Knowles, Barton, and Mark Goddard."

"Can I have a word?" Calladine asked. "In private."

Greco followed him into the corridor. "Why the long face, Tom? It's a successful conclusion. I thought you'd be pleased."

"Oh I am, but I don't believe Noah Crosby's death had anything to do with this case."

That stopped Greco in his tracks. "Want to explain?"

"Just put it down to instinct," Calladine said. "I need to check out a couple of things, but I should have the answer before the end of the day. And you should know that Lena is denying having anything to do with Mark's murder."

"Do you believe her?" Greco asked.

"I'm not sure. Let's just say I'm thinking about it."

"What's up?" Ruth asked when he went back inside.

"Nothing, but I've got to go out."

"We're about to celebrate in the Wheatsheaf, but if you want me to come along, I will."

"No, you lot go and have that drink. If I get this sorted in time, I'll join you."

"I know you. Something's up. Want to tell me about it?"

He stuck his hand in his pocket and handed Ruth a couple of twenty pound notes. "Perhaps later. Have the first one on me."

Calladine left them to it. He wanted a word with Julian before he acted on his suspicions.

* * *

"I was about to leave for the day," Julian grumbled. "Some of us do have lives outside of work."

That was rich coming from him. Julian lived for his work, although that did seem to have moderated since Maisie had come along. "The paint flecks on Alfie Lovell's clothing, has anything come up?"

"I've been working on that for most of the day. They are a match for the transit you brought in from Goddard's garden centre. I also found debris on his jumper the same as on the tyres, compost for example."

"In your opinion it was the transit that hit him?"

Julian nodded. "Yes, but the big question you have to ask is who was driving."

"Mostly the vehicle was used by Barton, but others who worked at the centre used it too."

"When it was searched, a cigarette end was found in the driver's footwell. I have run tests and it has Noah Crosby's DNA on it."

Calladine knew that Noah hung around with Barton, was part of his so-called gang. "Is there any way of knowing when that cigarette end was dropped?"

"I'm afraid not, Tom."

Calladine didn't doubt now that Alfie had been hit by Goddard's transit and it was possible that Noah had been driving. If not him then Barton. "Would any of the technicians working here recall the Shadow case from years ago?"

"No, Tom, too long ago."

He thanked Julian and went back to his car. He had confirmation of the vehicle but there was more information out there, he was sure of it. Next on his list was Killian Seddon.

* * *

Killian was at home, in one of his sullen moods. He glowered at Calladine while his mother did all the talking.

"I was out of my mind with worry and you lot weren't any help. In the end he came home himself. He's not said where he went though, and I'm worried sick. He could have got himself mixed up in anything."

"Want to talk to me?" Calladine asked him. "Clearly something has been bothering you and the sooner we sort it the better."

But the lad remained stubbornly silent. He grabbed a can of soft drink from the kitchen and flopped on the sofa.

"Is this to do with Noah?" Calladine asked. "D'you have information about what happened to him?"

On hearing the words Killian flushed beetroot red and slammed the can down on the table. "You haven't a clue. If I'd said anything at the time he'd have got me too. Ever since he did Noah he's been watching me. He's everywhere I go and I'm sick of it."

His mother looked puzzled. She sat beside her son and took his hand. "Barton's dead, love. He can't hurt you."

"Your mum's right, Killian. We've made several arrests. The people who killed Barton and Knowles are under lock and key."

Killian turned to Calladine. "I'm not talking about Barton or any of his gang. This one works in the shadows."

CHAPTER FIFTY-SEVEN

An odd choice of words but they sent a shiver down Calladine's spine. Nonetheless, Killian had been helpful. He might not have given him a name — fair enough, the lad was terrified — but what he had said was enough for Calladine.

Calladine returned to his car and made for home. It was almost six in the evening and with luck Ken Lovell would still be at his place finishing the decorating. Calladine believed that Lovell was the key to it all, but he had a bad feeling. The man was withdrawn, kept his feelings hidden and if his instincts were correct, he was dangerous.

He was in luck. Lovell's van was still outside his cottage. The front door was open. Lovell was carrying out his ladders.

"All done, Mr Calladine. I haven't written out a bill yet but I'll drop it off sometime tomorrow. Got to rush, Babs is in a panic about a leaky tap at home." He put the ladders in the back of his van and was about to climb into the driving seat when Calladine stopped him.

"Hang on a minute, Ken. I've got a couple of questions."

"What? About the cost of the job?"

"No, about the murder of Noah Crosby."

Lovell looked puzzled. "You've sorted that. I heard something on the local news about arrests being made."

"Not for Noah, or the attack on Barton before he was murdered."

"I know nothing about that."

"I think you do, Ken. I think you know exactly what happened to Noah."

Ken Lovell stared at Calladine for a few moments as if considering his next words carefully. Finally, he closed the van doors and locked them. "He was a nasty little insect who had no respect for anything." Lovell spat the words angrily. "I did my homework, which was more than you lot did. You never even spoke to the kids."

"We tried, Ken. Problem was they wouldn't speak to us."

"The Crosby lad was driving the vehicle that killed my boy. Him behind the wheel and Barton in the passenger seat. They were racing round the estate, came roaring round one of the tower blocks and mowed down my Alfie without a second thought. They didn't even stop."

"You murdered Noah, Ken. You should have come to us with any evidence you had. We'd have investigated, got to the truth."

"Piss off! You lot weren't interested. The kids knew — the likes of that Seddon boy, he saw it happen."

"Did you put pressure on Killian to speak to you?"

"Too bloody true I did. In the end I couldn't shut him up. D'you know, one of his grubby little friends actually has the moment of impact on his mobile?"

If only whoever that was had confided in the police. "You'll have to come with me," Calladine said. "You can't have believed you'd get away with it."

Lovell shrugged. "I don't really care. Here, you take the van keys. Babs will get her brother to move it. You can settle up with her too."

"One thing still puzzles me, why the Shadow, Ken? How did you know about him?"

"He was a killer from round here, something of a mystery, and that appealed. I'd been told about him by a friend in the nick I visit from time to time. You'll know him too, Mark Goddard. Him and the Shadow share a cell."

That caused Calladine some surprise on two fronts. First, that Ken knew Goddard well enough to visit him and second, that the Shadow was actually banged up. All these years and he'd been under the impression that he'd got away with it. "What did they get him on in the end?"

"Not murder. Serious fraud, I think. But he didn't take kindly to Mark telling me his identity. Challenged him about it, said that Mark had betrayed him and that he'd suffer. The man might have been dangerous once but these days he's off his head on heroin most of the time."

"Heroin? Where does he get it from?"

Ken gave him an old-fashioned look. "C'mon, Mr Calladine. You know as well as I do how lax security can be in those places. It's not hard if you pay well enough and know the right people."

EPILOGUE

Wednesday

"How did you know it was Lovell?" Ruth asked the next morning. "And don't just go off on your own like that again to arrest a killer. Anything could have happened."

"Lovell's not a killer. He wanted revenge for his lad. He was driven to do what he did by grief."

"Nonetheless he's made a statement, admitted everything. Killing Noah, the attack on Barton. He held nothing back. Rocco and I interviewed him and I got the impression that us finally knowing was a relief."

Calladine sipped on his tea. "Yes, I can believe that. In a roundabout way he was also responsible for the murder of Mark Goddard, the Shadow's last victim, I hope."

"That means Lena was telling you the truth about that. She didn't arrange to have her husband killed."

"I misjudged her, but given it's Lena we're dealing with, an easy mistake to make."

"Well that's something at least. We can all breathe easily knowing that the Shadow isn't back in reality, but locked up tight in prison. Surely we can find out his identity now and get justice for his victims."

"That is being looked into as we speak. Anyway, I've got to go out," Calladine said. "Greco comes looking, tell him I'm tidying up some loose ends."

"What loose ends? As far as I can see there aren't any."

"Kitty."

"Oh, you mean a personal loose end. That's different."

"She's still living at hers and I'd like to know where our relationship is going, if anywhere."

"Buy her flowers and take her out for dinner tonight."

But it wasn't that simple. Kitty wanted a lot more from him than that. For a while now, Calladine had suspected that what she really wanted was commitment and that scared him. There was Amy and his feelings for her for a start.

At this time of the day, Kitty would be in her office. He left the car at the station and made his way up the High Street on foot. What to say to her? How should he play this? Ruth was right about the flowers and stuff, he needed to do some serious grovelling, but he'd sort that later. For now they needed to talk, and he must apologise. He'd practically ignored her since his return to work and it'd been her that had nursed him through his illness.

He pushed open the office door, having decided to tell her the truth. He wasn't ready for anything other than what they had currently — not yet. But he did want her to move back in. He missed her.

When he entered the room, Kitty was at her desk with her back to him, speaking on her mobile. Calladine was about to approach when she said to whoever she was talking to. "I've got to go now, Freddie, but I'll see you later for dinner." She laughed. "Okay, I'll pack a bag and stay at yours. I've spent so many nights with you lately that I'm thinking of moving in anyway."

Calladine felt sick, let down, but quickly realised it was his own fault. Kitty was younger than him and an attractive woman. He would have left there and then, said nothing, but she swivelled round in her office chair and saw him. Her face fell instantly.

"What can I say? I'm sorry you heard that, Tom. I did intend to tell you about Freddie but you've been so busy."

"Don't, Kitty, it's all right, there's no need for excuses. You've got someone else and I don't blame you. I'm a non-runner in the romance stakes. Work's back in the frame and that means my personal life suffers."

She handed him a door key. "It's a relief that you can take it so well. I've already collected my stuff from yours." She stood on tiptoe and kissed his cheek. "We're not right together anyway, and certainly not now that Amy's back on the scene."

Could she be right? Could he and Amy really try again? Calladine pocketed the key and left. That was the end of that, his interlude with Kitty was well and truly over.

He started to walk back to the station when someone called to him. It was Julian.

"I've been on an impromptu visit to the babe. Zoe thinks we should get her christened. What d'you think?"

"I'm easy. I'll go with the majority."

"That's what I thought you'd say. She wants Ruth and Jake to be godparents. It'll just be a family affair, two weeks Sunday. Free up the date and let Ruth know."

Calladine nodded. "Amy okay?"

"Yes, and asking after you. She said to tell you that the kettle's on. She seems to think you'll be in need of a little comfort."

"Did she say why?"

"You've split with Kitty, is that right?"

Calladine nodded. "Did Amy tell you that?"

Julian nodded.

"Rather, she's split with me." He stood watching the bustle of the High Street, the constant stream of traffic and the sound of people going about their business. "I think I'll take Amy up on the tea." He smiled. "See what other little gems she can tell me about my life at the moment."

THE END

ALSO BY HELEN H. DURRANT

Thank you for reading this book.

If you enjoyed it please leave feedback on Amazon or Goodreads, and if there is anything we missed or you have a question about, then please get in touch. We appreciate you choosing our book.

Founded in 2014 in Shoreditch, London, we at Joffe Books pride ourselves on our history of innovative publishing. We were thrilled to be shortlisted for Independent Publisher of the Year at the British Book Awards.

www.joffebooks.com

We're very grateful to eagle-eyed readers who take the time to contact us. Please send any errors you find to corrections@joffebooks.com. We'll get them fixed ASAP.